"Why are you flirting with me?"

John lowered his head. "I'll admit, at first it was because you rejected me."

She rolled her eyes. "I suppose it was the shock of that happening."

He looked up and laughed. "But then it was because you didn't expect compliments or gifts from me."

"And that was odd?"

"The women I know would sell their souls to snag a rich man. They're the kind my father usually marries. But they're not going to get me!"

So he was not the marrying kind. Still… "But I'm not exactly the type of woman to turn heads."

"You are to me. Since I've met you, you occupy my mind most of the time."

Diane tugged on her suit lapels. "You're flirting again, Mr. Davis. It's not appropriate at a business lunch. Don't you respect me?"

"Absolutely." He leaned in close and whispered on a husky breath, "But I also want to sleep with you."

Dear Reader,

Long ago, when I was young (ha!) I began my career by writing Regencies. I enjoyed writing heroines who looked for love in life, rather than position, fortune and fame. *The Marrying Kind* is like a Regency in that my characters are *not* looking for marriage. Or at least they think they aren't! This attractive, successful and cynical man is about to meet his match in an independent and wary woman.

I really enjoyed writing these two characters. They are a little different from what I usually write, but a little change is good, isn't it? However, you may notice that I can't seem to stop bringing people together in a type of family.

I think we all try to create a family around us, whether by blood or circumstances. This is the second book of my DALLAS DUETS series, which takes place in a fourplex on Yellow Rose Lane. We've got one more story to tell, *Mommy for a Minute*, which will be out in August. I hope you'll look for that story, too! Dallas is a very nice place to visit.

If you have comments or questions, you can visit me at my Web site, www.judychristenberry.com.

Happy reading!

Judy Christenberry

Judy Christenberry
THE MARRYING KIND

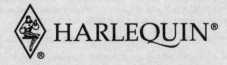

HARLEQUIN®

TORONTO • NEW YORK • LONDON
AMSTERDAM • PARIS • SYDNEY • HAMBURG
STOCKHOLM • ATHENS • TOKYO • MILAN • MADRID
PRAGUE • WARSAW • BUDAPEST • AUCKLAND

ISBN-13: 978-0-373-75165-5
ISBN-10:   0-373-75165-6

THE MARRYING KIND

www.eHarlequin.com

Printed in U.S.A.

ABOUT THE AUTHOR

Judy Christenberry has been writing romances for over fifteen years because she loves happy endings as much as her readers do. A former French teacher, Judy now devotes herself to writing full-time. She hopes readers have as much fun with her stories as she does. She spends her spare time reading, watching her favorite sports teams and keeping track of her two daughters. Judy lives in Texas.

Books by Judy Christenberry

HARLEQUIN AMERICAN ROMANCE

878—STRUCK BY THE TEXAS MATCHMAKERS†
885—RANDALL PRIDE*
901—TRIPLET SECRET BABIES
918—RANDALL RICHES*
930—RANDALL HONOR*
950—RANDALL WEDDING*
969—SAVED BY A TEXAS-SIZED WEDDING†
1000—A RANDALL RETURNS*
1033—REBECCA'S LITTLE SECRET**
1058—RACHEL'S COWBOY**
1073—A SOLDIER'S RETURN**
1097—A TEXAS FAMILY REUNION**
1117—VANESSA'S MATCH**
1133—A RANDALL THANKSGIVING
1145—DADDY NEXT DOOR‡

*Brides for Brothers
†Tots for Texans
**Children of Texas
‡Dallas Duets

Chapter One

"Dad, I don't need another woman pawing over me. I've got enough women already trying to figure out how to get me to marry them."

"Son, this one is different. Her mother promised me—"

"Come on, Dad, you know women. They'll promise you their souls if it'll get them your charge cards."

"John, I'm only asking for one evening. She's a good-looking blonde. Surely you can spare one night. For me."

John stared at his father. He loved him, even if he didn't agree with his choices, especially about women.

But what the hell. He could endure one evening with another money-hungry female. He'd done it often enough. He'd sit through one gourmet dinner while she ordered the most expensive meal and prattled inanely for two hours. Then he'd take her home and he'd be finished.

"Okay, Dad, I'll take her out once. If I don't like her, that's it, okay?"

"Thank you, John." His father handed him a piece of paper. "Here's the address. She lives in a fourplex on Yellow Rose Lane."

DIANE BLACK MOVED ABOUT the downstairs apartment in the fourplex on Yellow Rose Lane, watering the various plants.

"Oh, you poor dear. You've suffered a lot, haven't you? I'm so sorry I didn't get to you yesterday."

There'd been too much work to do. She'd left the bank about nine, even later than usual, working up a proposal for a potential client she'd been pursuing for weeks. A few hours on her laptop catching up on investments were followed by some light reading in bed—a trade magazine of financial projections. She'd fallen asleep with the magazine on her chest, never thinking of the plants she'd been asked to tend.

She poured water into the dry soil of one dieffenbachia. "Here's a little extra for you," she crooned. She pinched off a dead leaf or two before moving on to the next plant, talking to it as much as she had the last one.

She was usually quiet, but she blossomed when she talked to the plants. She had a large collection in her own apartment and had promised her friend and neighbor, Jennifer, to take care of her plants, too, while she was on her honeymoon.

When a knock sounded on the front door, Diane wondered who could be calling on the absent newlyweds and their children.

Should she answer it?

Another knock, this one more forceful, decided her.

She hurried to the door. Swinging it open, she stared at the six-foot-two, dark-haired hunk in front of her. "Hello?"

"I'm glad you finally answered. I was beginning to think you weren't home."

"I—"

"No, don't say it. Look, I promised my dad, as you promised your mother. So let's just get this evening over with so we can face them and tell them we've done as they asked. That's what we need to do."

"We do?" Diane blinked several times. She knew she was tired, but what he was saying didn't make sense.

The man reached forward and took her arm. "Come on. I've got a reservation at a nearby restaurant. It won't take that long. If we don't like each other, we can cut it short and still have done what we promised."

She pulled away from his hold. What was wrong with this guy, acting like an arrogant oaf? "You can't just—"

"Sure I can. I'm paying. Get your purse and let's go."

Of all the pompous, demanding egos! Just who did this guy think he was?

Then it hit her.

Could it be…?

Before she married Nick, Jennifer had told Diane that her mother was trying to set her up with a man of her so-called class. Meaning a rich guy. Could this be the man? In his designer suit, which fit him like a glove, he shouted money. He seemed just like someone Jennifer's mom would approve of.

"Excuse me," Diane said, "but there's obviously been a—"

"No time for that now," he said, reaching behind her to the hall stand and grabbing her purse. "We've got a table waiting."

"But—"

He put up a hand to halt her objection, and Diane saw red. No man was going to get away with treating her like this. She'd teach him a lesson.

She'd go along with him—and then zap him with the truth.

Smiling sweetly, she said, "I'll drive my own car and follow you."

"I don't see the need—" Then, as if the light dawned, he continued, "Oh, you're being cautious. In that case, fine. I'll go slow so you can follow."

He strode out the door, cradling her elbow the whole way. Did he think she couldn't walk on her own, or was he afraid she'd balk again?

As she drove behind him to the restaurant, Diane couldn't help but laugh when she envisioned one-upping the pompous rich guy. She knew it was rather evil, and totally out of character for her, but she couldn't resist the temptation to take this man down a peg. All her life she'd despised how a certain class of men treated women. And she should know; she was in the male-dominated banking industry.

As soon as she parked beside his Mercedes, he was at her door to open it, leaning down with his hand extended.

This had gone far enough, she thought. "We need to talk before we go in."

He led her out of the car. "Not here. It's too hot. We'll talk at our table." And he swept her into the four-star Dallas restaurant.

The maître d' obviously recognized him on sight. He was one up on her, Diane joked to herself. He led them to a private candlelit table and held out her chair.

With a sigh, she sat down. This little game had gone far enough, she decided. Her "date"—whoever he was— was going to be irate when she told him who *she* was.

"Now can we talk?" she asked, when the maître d' turned away.

But then the sommelier stepped up to the table, rattling off their specialty wines, aged to perfection.

"I don't drink," she told him when he'd finished his prepared speech.

Her dinner companion seemed surprised, then re-grouped. "In that case, we'll both have iced tea." The sommelier went away, dejected.

"I need to tell you something," she blurted, before anyone else interrupted them.

Her companion waved her off. "Nonsense. What we need to do is decide what we'll eat for dinner. There's plenty of time to talk after we order."

But her selection wasn't met with approval. When the waiter came, her companion smoothly overrode her decision and instead doubled his own three-course dinner.

"Very well, sir." The waiter nodded and quietly slipped away.

Her "date" clasped his well-manicured hands in front of him and speared her with a direct gaze. "Now, what was it that you couldn't wait to tell me, Jennifer?"

"I'm not Jennifer."

His eyes—blue like the deepest ocean—widened. Then he cleared his throat. "Then who are you?"

She lowered her own eyes, suddenly feeling a bit guilty. "I'm Diane Black, Jennifer's neighbor."

He unclasped his hands and lay them flat on the table. She looked up and saw the muscles bunch along his jaw as he clenched his teeth. "Don't you think you should have told me that before?"

Was he not there before, when she'd tried five or six times? "If you'll recall, you weren't exactly interested in letting me speak."

He didn't reply.

"Next time, maybe you'll let a woman get a word in every now and then." She grabbed her purse and stood up, ready to make a discreet exit.

But his voice halted her in place. "I don't like to eat alone."

She turned back to him. "You want me to stay?"

He nodded, but his eyes didn't soften.

She compared the thought of a mouthwatering steak to the can of soup that awaited her at home, and resumed her seat.

"Where is Jennifer?"

Diane couldn't repress a slight, lopsided grin as she revealed the irony. "She and her husband and their three daughters are on their honeymoon."

The man shrugged. "Not exactly the scenario I'd choose for my honeymoon."

"It's what Jennifer chose. She'd just adopted three little girls when she met her husband. They went to Walt Disney World for a week, then they're going on a cruise."

"I guess I was a little late following through with my dad's suggestion."

"I don't think it would've mattered. Jennifer wasn't interested in what her mother wanted for her. Even if you were Prince Charming, she wouldn't have gone out with you."

"But you didn't mind? Was it the money that convinced you?"

Diane bent over, picked up her purse and stood. She didn't have anything to say to this man. She got two feet from the table when he grabbed her arm.

"All right, I apologize. I'm sorry. I just don't like to be tricked."

"You also don't like to let people talk. I tried to explain many times."

"And I wouldn't let you."

"No, you wouldn't." She looked around for their waiter. "Why don't we ask to be put at two different tables? I needed to eat out this evening, anyway."

"Why did you need to eat out?"

"A rough day at the office," she said mildly.

"Want to tell me about it?"

"No, thank you. I remember Jen telling me about you, but I can't remember your name."

"I'm Jonathon Davis. You can call me John. Nice to meet you, Diane."

She offered a small smile. "Shall I wave to the waiter so he can find me another table?"

"No, definitely not. I told you I don't like to eat alone. Why shouldn't we get to know each other and enjoy our meal?"

She hesitated, then said, "Okay, but I'll pay for my dinner."

"I thought you knew I was wealthy?"

"What difference does that make? I'm not exactly on welfare!"

He leaned toward her. "I invited you, so I pay."

"But I accepted under false pretenses."

"I think that was my fault. Please?"

She lowered her gaze. His eyes were magnetic. "I—I suppose. Okay."

"I haven't had to work this hard to share dinner with a lady in a long time."

She just shook her head. She didn't know what to say to that comment.

"So tell me what kind of job you have."

"I'm a banker."

"You work in a bank? Are you a secretary or a teller?"

"I'm vice president in charge of investments."

"Oh, sorry. I didn't know they gave those kind of jobs to women."

"They don't. I earned it!" Diane had faced enough discrimination in the workplace, she didn't need it from a dinner companion. This time when she stood, she didn't give him a chance to stop her. She scooped up her purse and stormed from the restaurant.

HE'D BLOWN IT.

It hadn't been his intention to send her running. He'd simply said what had come to mind.

Diane Black was unlike his other dinner dates, who dabbled in careers or made one out of fund-raising for charities and planning socialite balls. She was a working woman, and he didn't know how to act around that ilk.

Besides, she had only given him what he deserved. He had been a bear, dragging her along to dinner, too intent on getting it over with to really listen to what she'd been trying to say.

He sighed, staring at her empty seat. He truly hated eating alone.

An idea formed. He asked the waiter to wrap up their meals, and left him a sizable tip.

Fifteen minutes later, he arrived back at the fourplex. As he pulled into the parking lot, he was pleased to see Diane's car. Now all he had to figure out was which apartment was hers.

He reached the door with his stack of take-out boxes just as the door was shoved opened and four very attractive young women came out. One of them stopped to stare at John.

"Hello. Are you lost?"

"No. I'm here to see Diane."

"Oh. Well, she's home. She came in a few minutes ago."

"Which one is she in?"

"Upstairs on the right."

"Thanks." He hurried up the steps.

Knocking on the appropriate door, he waited until it opened, then grinned, holding up the redolent boxes. "Hi. I brought dinner."

Diane didn't return the smile. "No, thank you. I'm fixing dinner already."

"Come on, Diane. There's no point in letting this go to waste."

She glanced down and drew in a deep breath, the delicious aroma breaking her resolve. "Fine. Which ones belong to me?"

"Oh, no, you don't. Either I come in with the boxes or they don't come in."

"Fine," she said again. But instead of opening the door wider, she closed it and he heard the lock click into place.

"Diane! Diane, you're not being fair. Come on, open the door."

He was answered with silence.

"Diane, I want to have dinner with you. I've already paid for it. The least you can do is share it with me."

After a few minutes of banging on her door and calling out to her, to no avail, he returned to his car. He sat there in the car eating his meal…and hers, too. But he saw no sign of her.

Finally, he drove home, questioning why he had hung around waiting for her to acknowledge him. He had a lot of women after him, didn't he? So why had he waited for her to forgive him?

He hadn't found an answer by the time he reached home. The housekeeper greeted him, wanting to know if he needed a snack before he went to bed.

"No, Mrs. Walker, thank you. I hope you didn't wait up for me."

"No, of course not, Mr. Davis. I hadn't gone to bed yet."

He smiled at her and continued up the stairs. Of course she hadn't gone to bed. It was only eight o'clock. What was wrong with him?

Tomorrow would be a different day. He could face his father without feeling guilty. And he wouldn't have to explain that his date had been the one to call a halt to the evening.

Maybe that was what bothered him more than anything. She hadn't wanted him! Most of the women after him wanted him because of his wealth, of course, but even that didn't tempt Diane.

Had he gotten lazy? John didn't think he'd ever angered a woman enough that she gave him up. But maybe he needed to be more careful about how he treated women. He certainly hadn't learned that from his father, who was currently on wife number five, a woman younger than John.

With a sigh, he entered the master suite and began undressing. He'd get in bed and watch some television. That would take his mind off the infuriating Diane Black.

Sure it would.

DIANE STUDIED HER wardrobe the next morning. It was full of black and gray suits—what she'd learned early on constituted professional dress for a banker, male or female. The only color was an occasional muted pastel blouse. Today she actually yearned for a red jacket.

Maybe she'd go shopping tonight. After all, her position was safe, wasn't it? She could occasionally break the rules if she still looked professional.

She didn't want to question the sudden need to stand out. That would force her to think about the aggravating man she'd met last night. John Davis had irritated her more than anyone she'd ever met. Especially when she remembered that her bank, quite a large institution, had backed several of his recent projects.

Of course, he hadn't recognized her, because she wasn't involved in loans. So he wouldn't know how to get in touch with her. And that was for the best.

She dressed in a pearl-gray suit with a silk blouse in silvery tones. It was one of her favorite outfits, and she needed her spirits lifted.

When she reached the bank, she was her normal quiet self, calm and pleasant. Her blond hair was pinned back neatly, the only nod to femininity her discreet silver earrings.

Once she was seated behind her desk, Diane relaxed and began her normal routine. She loved her job and understood how important it was for her customers.

In fact, today she was taking one of her clients to lunch. Mrs. Winthrop was a dear. Her husband had made a fortune, but since his death ten years ago Mrs.

Winthrop had been relying on Diane to keep the fortune intact so as to provide for her grandchildren.

Diane was making sure that she didn't invest the woman's money in any risky stocks. She wanted the same thing as Mrs. Winthrop.

In fact, she had some projections to run before lunch. It was time to focus on the people who mattered.

And get her mind off John Davis.

OKAY, SO THE ARRIVAL of morning hadn't removed Diane Black from his mind. John dressed for work, thinking about the woman who'd rejected him last evening. But it wasn't because she'd dumped him. About midnight he'd finally admitted that he'd brought that rejection on himself. He'd been arrogant.

He'd complimented women all his life. It was how he got around them, got them to do what he wanted. But he'd been angry last night. He'd tried to force her to his will. And been irritated when she hadn't done as he'd wanted.

Guilt had washed through him when he realized it. He felt like an insensitive clod stomping on a delicate flower. He wanted to apologize.

So, after he reached his office, he took out a phone book and began calling all the small banks, asking for a VP named Diane Black. By lunchtime, he'd had no luck. Had she lied to him?

If she had, it was his fault. He'd made it impossible for her to admit to having a lowly position.

Maybe his personal banker would know where Diane

was. He was having lunch with Mark Golan today to discuss a new project for which he needed funding.

While he'd always handled his projects successfully, John wanted to be sure he had all his ducks in a row. So he put Diane from his mind and gathered up the various drawings and charts for his presentation. That was one thing he had learned from his father—to be the consummate professional. His personal life might be a wreck, but not his business life.

Which meant his father had the money to pay for all his mistakes, in the form of alimony for each of his three former wives. John's mother, his dad's first wife, had died when John was a little boy.

He had no intention of repeating his father's mistakes. He wouldn't be turned by a pretty face, which were a dime a dozen for a wealthy man. Too many women looked for a meal ticket they could marry.

He shook his head. Time to clear his mind from thoughts of Diane or his father. He needed to concentrate on business.

He met Mark at a nearby restaurant. Over lunch they talked about sports and mutual acquaintances. John knew the drill. He wouldn't talk about his project until they arrived back at Guaranty National Bank, the largest and most respected financial institution in the Dallas area.

As he stepped into Mark Golan's office, impeccably appointed to befit a VP, he began organizing his thoughts in his head. He didn't want to make any mistakes in his presentation.

An hour later, after his pitch, it was with relief that he

heard the bank's decision—approval of the loan he wanted to finance the work. He was surprised to find Diane returning to his thoughts almost immediately. How had she gotten such control over his mind?

"John, you did a great presentation," Mark said after the senior members had left his office. "You made us both look good."

"Glad to hear it. You've always been good to me, Mark. I wouldn't want to let you down."

"It's mutual. If I can ever do anything for you, just let me know."

"Well, there is something…." John tried to affect a casual attitude. "You pretty much know most of the banking community, don't you?"

"Sure. I've worked at a couple of different banks, plus we're all members of a professional group. Are you looking for someone? I hope you're not thinking of leaving me," he joked.

"No, of course not. But I met someone who said she was a VP in charge of investments. I figured she meant in a small bank. After all, I don't think you have too many female bankers."

Mark's eyebrows rose. "Careful, buddy. You sound way out of touch with today's world if you think that way."

"Really? How many female bankers do you have?"

"I believe we're up to fourteen now, including a VP in charge of investments."

John froze. Then he cleared his throat. "Don't tell me her name is Diane Black?"

Chapter Two

"How'd you know?" Mark sounded skeptical.

"I, uh, recently met her and wanted to—to see her again." Damn it, when was the last time he'd stuttered, talking about a woman? It must've been twenty years ago, when he was twelve and had a crush on Darlene Carey in the seventh grade.

Mark looked upset. "Oh, no! You're going to cost me my job. You keep away from Diane."

"What are you talking about?" John demanded.

Though only thirty-four, Mark sounded every bit the wise old sage when he said, "John, you're a great businessman, but you cut a wide swath through the women in Dallas. Even us staid bankers know how often you change girlfriends. And you never offer them marriage."

"No, I don't. I'm not my father!"

"I didn't mean to imply you were, John. But don't mess with Diane. She's not your type and I don't want her to get hurt."

"I'm not going to hurt her. I just want to visit with her for a few minutes. Surely you can't object to that."

"Why?"

"Why what?"

"Why do you want to visit with her?"

"If you must know, I was rude to her last night over a misunderstanding, and I owe her an apology."

"That's all?"

"Yeah, that's all. Now, do I need a note from my mother to get to see her?" He figured Mark heard his sarcasm. John wasn't trying to hide his displeasure.

"Yeah, okay, but remember, you promised not to hurt her."

"I remember."

"Her office is on the third floor. Just follow the signs to the investment department."

"Thanks, I will." John strode out of Mark's office and headed directly for the elevator. When he got off on the third floor, he realized he was almost running. He stopped and drew a deep breath. No need to advertise his eagerness to see her. Instead he adopted a casual stroll down the hall.

When he entered the investments area, he was greeted by a receptionist.

"I'd like to see Diane Black," he told her.

"Ms. Black has someone with her right now, but you're free to wait, Mr...."

"Davis. John Davis. And yes, I'll wait."

He sat down on the sofa across from the reception-ist's desk and picked up a magazine from the coffee table. He flipped through it, paying little attention to the contents.

His attention zeroed in, however, when he saw an elderly woman exit one of the bank offices and heard the receptionist on the intercom. "A Mr. Davis to see you."

Diane's voice came back through the intercom, curt and clipped. "Please tell Mr. Davis he has the wrong department. Loans are on the first floor."

John started walking toward Diane's office, despite the receptionist's protests. "Sir, you can't just walk in on Ms. Black. Sir—"

By that time, he had opened the door to her office. "Will you tell that young woman to stop yelling at me?"

Diane sent him an angry look, but pushed down the intercom button. "Wendy, it's all right. I forgot that Mr. Davis needed to talk to me about something."

"What do I need to talk to you about?" he asked.

"I have no idea, but I don't want Wendy to feel she failed me."

"That's very kind of you, Diane. And I'm trying to be kind, too."

"How are you doing that?"

"I was rude and arrogant last night and I wanted to apologize to you."

"I see. Yes, that's very kind of you. Thank you."

He continued to stand there, staring at her.

"Is there anything else?"

"You could ask me to sit down."

"Why?"

Why did people keep asking him that question? He wondered. First Mark, now her.

Before he could reply, Diane moved to the door. "I see no need for additional conversation, John, so perhaps it would be best if you leave."

He deliberately sat down. "Perhaps I should remind you that I do a lot of business with this bank."

"That's not necessary, Mr. Davis. I'm well aware of your past history with *my* bank. I'll be glad to refer you to whoever you need to talk to to be sure your needs are met."

"And what if you're the one I need to see?"

"For what reason?"

"I told you. I needed to apologize to you."

"I appreciate that, but you've already done so."

"So you're throwing me out?"

"Mr. Davis, I'm pointing out—rightly, I think—that I'm at work. It is not a social situation. If you have something about my job that you need to discuss, so be it. But if not, then yes, I'm throwing you out."

"All right, I'll go, on one condition."

"And what is that?"

"Have dinner with me tonight so I can show you I'm a changed man."

"So you think forcing me to have dinner with you will show me you're no longer arrogant? Isn't that being arrogant again?"

He nodded, conceding the point. "Well, you've definitely proved one thing."

"What's that?"

"You're much brighter than most women I've met."

She glared at him, saying nothing.

"You don't consider that a compliment?" he asked.

"No, I don't. Your scorn for my gender is disgusting."

"My scorn? I was simply being honest."

She opened the door further. "I have nothing more to say to you, Mr. Davis."

"So you *are* throwing me out?"

"Yes, I am." She spoke clearly and precisely, leaving no doubt.

"So it's arrogant to give you credit for your brains?"

"No, it's arrogant for you to think you can determine a woman's brilliance. How do you rate men?"

He frowned. "Most of the men I work with are fairly intelligent."

"But the women are not?"

"I don't usually deal with women in my business. I mean, I'm a developer and builder. It almost always involves men."

"Well, Mr. Davis, in case you don't know it, there are a lot of intelligent women out there."

"I've met some of them, but they aren't using their brains to get to me. They use their bodies, and I don't think they're smart."

"I agree. Now, if you'll excuse me?"

"No dinner?"

"No dinner."

He sighed. "Okay. Maybe another day."

She kept her expression impassive and merely stood there, waiting for him to leave.

Without another word John returned to Mark's office.

"Did you see her?" his banker asked, worry creasing his brow.

"Yeah, I saw her. How about you set up a dinner so I can talk to her?"

"Why didn't you *ask* her to dinner, if that's what you want?"

"I did. But she refused. She'll only consider going out if it's for business reasons."

"In other words, you're asking me to trick her? No way, John. Diane wouldn't like that."

"No, not lie to her. I'm prepared to invest a million dollars through her."

"You are? Why?"

"I'm getting very tired of that question. I want to be sure I won't ever go broke. So I'm going to make a sizable investment."

"That's a good idea, John. I'm sure Diane will be happy about it, too."

"Can you just tell her a client wants to invest a million without giving her my name? And have her meet you at a restaurant?"

"I suppose so." Mark stopped short and his eyes narrowed. "You're not going to back out on the investment, are you?"

"No, I'm not."

"Okay. What night is good for you?"

"What's wrong with tonight?"

"I don't know if my wife can find a sitter that soon."

"Call her and see," John suggested.

After a brief phone conversation, during which

Mark's wife promised to try to line up a sitter and let him know if she was successful, John agreed to call Mark in an hour.

Then he left the bank, wondering what had come over him. The idea of investing had been in his mind before, but it hadn't occurred to him lately, until he'd met Diane Black.

DIANE LOOKED UP when her computer indicated a new e-mail had arrived. She reached for the curser and clicked it open. It was from one of the vice presidents in the loan department, indicating he had a client who wanted to invest a million dollars. She raised an eyebrow.

Then she typed in, Sure, I'd love to meet with your client. When do you want to set it up? Lunch?

The answer appeared almost at once. He wanted to meet this evening. I think it would be good before he changes his mind. Is that okay with you?

Yes. Give me a time and a place, she typed in, and hit Send. After she received the information she needed, she turned off her computer. It was already past closing.

It was only after she was in her car, heading home, that she realized she hadn't asked the client's name. It occurred to her that John Davis could be the client, but she dismissed the thought. Mark wouldn't introduce her to someone who didn't intend to invest.

They were going to a nice restaurant, so Diane hurriedly changed into a simple black dress that she felt good in. She put on diamond ear studs, a reward she'd purchased for herself after her last promotion.

When she glanced in the mirror, she nodded to her image. She appeared festive, but conservative. Pleased with how she looked, she hurried back down to her car. She had fifteen minutes to get to the restaurant.

Mark and his wife were sitting at a table when she entered. Diane smiled. She'd met Elizabeth several times and liked her.

The maître d' led her to the table and held her chair for her. She greeted the Golans and immediately said, "I forgot to ask your client's name. Have I met him?"

Mark opened his mouth to answer and then stopped, his gaze going to a point over Diane's shoulder.

She turned to find what had grabbed his attention. And discovered John Davis reaching for the chair beside her. She said nothing to John, but turned and stared at her colleague, waiting for an explanation.

"I swear, Diane, John promised he wants to invest a million dollars. I wouldn't mislead you."

After a considering look, she nodded, but still didn't glance at John.

"Good evening, Diane. You look lovely tonight."

"Thank you," she replied coolly.

"You, too, Elizabeth. You look much better than you did the last time I saw you," John said with a grin.

Diane turned to stare at him. "That's rude."

"No, it's not," Elizabeth said. "We were on a picnic and the baby threw up all over me. I tried to clean up, but there wasn't much I could do. Everyone did their best to avoid me."

"Oh, you poor dear. Was she very sick?" Since

Diane had had no children or siblings, she knew little about babies.

Elizabeth laughed again. "No. She must've eaten something she didn't like. Little ones tend to throw up frequently."

Diane looked horrified.

"Haven't you ever been around babies?" John asked.

"No." After a moment she looked at him cautiously. "Have you?"

"Each of my stepmothers had an 'heir' to cement her marriage with my father. I never did any babysitting, but I was home more than my stepmothers, so I saw the nanny deal with a lot."

"A nanny? Your stepmothers didn't—No, I guess not." After composing herself, Diane said, "So, you have four brothers and sisters?"

"No, just three brothers. But I expect to be informed of another one on the way at any time." John looked at her. "You don't have any siblings?"

"No. I was a mistake they didn't want to repeat," she said, and then regretted her words. "Forget I said that. Now, you want to put a million dollars in my hands to invest?"

"Yes. I think you'll do a great job for me."

"I need to know what you expect. I can't promise gains by leaps and bounds, but I can guarantee growth. Is that what you're looking for?"

"Of course. I simply want to put that much money aside so I'll never go broke. It's a safeguard."

"Where is the money now?"

"It's in an account."

Diane stared at him, a slight frown on her face. Something didn't seem right. "Have you made investments before?"

"Yes, several times, but I've lost money, too. I think it's better for a professional to handle my investments instead of me trying to do that as well as handle my business projects."

While Diane couldn't argue with that logic, she proceeded with caution. "We'll need to discuss the kind of investments you have an interest in," she said slowly.

John nodded and flashed her a wide smile. "But first, why don't we order some drinks?"

After the waiter took their requests, Diane hesitated returning to the subject of John's investments. She'd been in the business long enough to develop a sixth sense about a potential client.

This time that sense was telling her to run as far and as fast as she could.

JOHN WAS AMAZED at how much trouble he'd gone to to convince Diane they should… Should what? Become business partners? Friends? Lovers?

Yeah, that was what he wanted. Even though she wasn't a beauty at first glance, not playing up her natural assets, the longer he knew her, the more beautiful she became.

He wanted to take out the pins holding back her long blond hair, and run his hands through it. He wanted to hold her against him, to feel her breathe, to kiss her just below her ear. To inhale her subtle scent. He wasn't sure why she appealed to him so much. Maybe it was because she wasn't chasing him. In fact, she seemed downright elusive.

That remark she'd made about her parents made him eager to question her about her childhood. The two of them might have a lot in common.

Throughout the evening he watched her carefully. Her every move was so graceful, nearly poetic. He wondered why she was alone.

That thought stopped him. *Was* she alone? There could be a man in her life. What would John do if there was?

At a pause in the conversation, he asked her, "Should we have invited your, uh, significant other?"

She lowered her eyes. "No, that's not necessary."

"Because there isn't anyone?" he pressed.

Her eyes speared him with a sharp look. "Because it has nothing to do with our conversation!"

Mark immediately intervened. "No, of course not. This is a business dinner. It's a chance to discuss your investment strategy with the professional you're giving the opportunity to handle your money."

"Of course," John agreed. He knew Diane wasn't going to make it a social situation. He was beginning to wonder if she even had a social life.

Abruptly, he said, "Do you snow ski, Diane?"

She stared at him. "In Texas? I don't think that ever happens."

"But Colorado's not that far away. Maybe you go there on vacation?"

"No, I haven't tried skiing."

"I go several times a year."

"We went last year and took the kids," Mark interjected. "We hired a high school student to come help with them."

"That was my idea," Elizabeth pointed out. "I didn't want to stay in the room and take care of the kids while Mark went skiing every day."

"Yeah. Sometimes I forget children require so much work, but Elizabeth reminds me by going off shopping on a Saturday. By the time she gets home, I'm desperate to get out of there," Mark assured them.

"Elizabeth is a great mother. Not every woman is. My father seems to have a talent of picking wives without that quality."

"You think it's something a woman is born with?" Diane asked.

"Oh, yeah. And pity the poor kids who have the wrong mother." John grinned at her.

"I don't agree," Elizabeth said. "I had to learn to be a good mother. I had friends who helped me, and my mom. She taught me a lot."

"I agree," Diane said. "They even offer parenting classes for those who doubt their abilities."

John seemed unconvinced. "Yeah, but you have to be interested in learning. My stepmothers only wanted a child to ensure that they got more money when the divorce came along."

"You're assuming they went into the marriage knowing it would end in divorce," Diane commented.

"Honey, my dad's famous for his marital problems.

He chooses a woman by her beauty. He keeps her until she turns into a wife and bugs him about things he doesn't want to do. That's when he discovers she's not the woman for him. By that time, a baby has come along, and the alimony and child support payments soon follow."

"That's a very cynical outlook, John," Diane protested.

"I'll have to introduce you to my father. Then you'll understand."

Annoyed, she turned to Elizabeth, looking for some safer conversation. "How old are your kids now?"

"One and a half, four and six."

"They must require a lot of energy," Diane guessed. "My friend Jennifer Carpenter—now Jennifer Barry—adopted three little girls close to those ages."

"Three at once?" Elizabeth asked, her voice rising. "How brave of her!"

"Yes, but they're so sweet. The three are sisters who were split up when their parents died. They're so glad to be back together now."

"Oh, yes, that's wonderful," Elizabeth said, tearing up just a little. "I can't imagine my children being separated."

Mark reached for his wife's hand. "That won't happen, honey. Remember, your sister and her husband said they'd take care of our kids if anything happens to us."

Diane watched the tender way Mark looked at his wife, and it made her heart ache. What would it be like to have someone who understood, who cared, who prepared for the future?

Elizabeth straightened her spine. "I'm sorry, Diane. Sometimes I worry."

"No need to apologize!" she exclaimed. "I found myself tearing up over my neighbor's little girls. I'm just glad they found such a great home."

John joined the conversation. "So Jennifer is a good mother?"

"Yes. She wasn't sure she would be, so she took a parenting class. But she's doing fine."

Mark looked at John. "You sound like you know her?"

"I know about her. My father wanted to set me up with her."

"She sounds like a catch," Mark said. "Why'd you refuse?"

"Actually, I didn't. I was too late. That's how I met Diane."

"Yes," Diane hurried to add. "And it was a mistake."

John turned to her, a smile dancing on his lips. "But not one I regret."

Chapter Three

How could she be alone with him?

The dilemma had kept Diane awake all night, and still plagued her this morning. She couldn't walk away from a million-dollar investor, yet she couldn't honestly accept John's invitation to lunch.

Last night, after his incendiary comment at dinner, he'd kept the conversation light and general—till he leaned in close to invite her to discuss his "portfolio" at lunch tomorrow. From the rumbling sound of his voice, she wondered what he really had in mind.

Maybe she'd invite Mark to join them. He'd be the perfect buffer to keep them on a strictly professional basis.

After she worked up some preliminary projections for John's investment, she called her coworker and made the offer. "I think John would be more at ease with another man there," she added, hoping that would seal the deal.

But Mark didn't fall for it. "I don't think so, Diane.

I got the idea he was determined to take you to lunch alone. He certainly didn't mention inviting me when we were together last night."

"He probably thought I would object, but I wouldn't, Mark. I promise." She fought to keep the desperation out of her voice.

"What's up with you two, anyway?"

Diane froze. "I don't know what you mean."

"I mean…well, why is he so determined to be with you, while you're so reluctant?"

"It's business, Mark, that's all."

"Well, I'm free for lunch, but you need to ask John if he wants me to come. If I don't hear from you, I'll know I was right."

"Fine," she conceded. "But I'm sure he'll change his mind." Then she hung up the phone.

"About what?" John asked, leaning against the open door to her office.

Diane gasped. Then she took a deep breath and said calmly, "Hi, John. You're a little early. I didn't expect you until noon." Since it was only eleven-thirty, he was actually a lot early.

"Were you talking about me?"

"Yes, I called Mark to see if he wanted to come with us."

John raised one eyebrow as she watched in fascination. "What did he say?"

"He said he didn't think you wanted him along."

"Smart man. Are you ready to go? I thought we should beat the lunch crowd."

"John, I don't mind if he comes, in case you don't like eating alone with me," Diane insisted.

"But I want to eat alone with you. I don't want Mark with us."

Just as she'd feared.

"By the way, you look great in that color, whatever it is."

"Th-thank you." The color was a rosy beige that no doubt paled in comparison to the blush on her cheeks now, thanks to his compliment. She'd deliberated over her choice of clothing for a long time that morning, finally settling on a black pinstripe suit and the pastel blouse she hardly ever wore.

"Are you ready?"

"Yes, but—All right, we'll go. I made a reservation for twelve o'clock."

"I know. I changed it to eleven-thirty."

Diane bent to get her purse, then stood. When she came around the desk, John took her hand.

"What are you doing?" she asked, snatching her arm away.

"I was holding your hand."

"I know, but I'm your banker, not…a woman." As soon as she said it, she knew it had come out all wrong. "I mean, I bet you don't hold Mark's hand."

He grinned, that white-toothed, wolfish smile. "No, I've never swung that way, honey. I'm strictly a ladies' man." He ushered her out of her office, whispering to her back, "And just for the record, Diane, you're all-woman."

HER CHEEKS STILL BURNED when they finally exited the building. She'd never been so grateful for fresh air.

"My car's right over there," she said, pointing to the left.

"Nope, we'll take mine," John said. "I know I'm being arbitrary, but I prefer to drive."

After pausing a moment, she gave in. That was easy to do, and it would please him. She might have to be stronger on things that mattered, so she should store up some good credit in the meantime.

When they reached the restaurant, the maître d' greeted them both by name. "I have your table ready. Right this way."

He led them to the most secluded table in the restaurant. Diane supposed it would be good for private business talk, but she didn't like feeling so isolated with John.

When they'd placed their orders, she launched right into business. "Now, I've laid out a plan—"

"Good. But I want to ask you something."

"Yes, of course," she agreed, thinking he wanted to ask about her philosophy in investing.

"Why did you say your parents considered you to be a mistake? Surely they don't think so now."

Diane just stared at him, aghast. She couldn't believe he'd asked such a personal question. No way would she answer it. Instead she began outlining her investment plans.

"Wait. You didn't answer my question."

"John, we're here to discuss investing."

"Look, I know about investing. I just don't have time

to do it myself. Invest half of it in quality stocks that will grow slowly. Invest a quarter in strong stocks that might go up or down, and monitor them closely. And with the rest of it, try a few flyers. Now can we talk about you?"

She blinked in surprise. "If you already knew what you wanted, why did we need to meet to discuss it?"

"Because I wanted to get to know you."

"But—"

"Isn't a million enough? I don't think I can pull out more right now, because I'm starting a new project, but—"

"John, you don't *pay* to get to know someone! That's outrageous!"

"But you seem resistant to the idea."

"But I'm not the kind of woman you like to date."

"I know, but I've gotten tired of those kind of women. Look, I asked about your parents because I think we may have something in common, that's all. Is that so bad?"

"No, of course not, but—" The conciliatory look on his face stopped her protest, softened her just enough. "Okay, you win. My parents are Alexander and Karen Black, quite famous archaeologists who teach at Southern Methodist University. They didn't intend to have children. I was an accident. They're very self-absorbed people. They hired someone to take care of me and, basically, abandoned me. I sometimes think I might've had a better life if they'd let someone adopt me when I was a baby."

"But aren't they proud of what you've achieved?"

She avoided John's intense blue gaze. "I doubt they

even know. They teach all year and travel all summer. I sometimes have Christmas dinner with them, unless they're having too big a party. Then they don't invite me."

John continued to stare at her. "That's it? Once a year? They don't call you?"

"No."

"Doesn't that hurt?"

"It used to, but I've come to accept it."

"But that's inhumane."

"No, they fed me and paid for someone to keep me safe. The nanny who stayed the longest…I keep in touch with her."

"How did you get through college?"

"I got to go to SMU free because they were such widely respected professors there. They gave me a small allowance above that. So I did just fine."

"I think I'd like to punch them in the nose," John snapped.

She didn't want to admit that his words meant anything to her, so she asked about his situation. "What about you? Where's your mother?"

"She died when I was four. Dad always says she was the love of his life, but I figure they would've divorced if she'd lived."

"You don't believe in love?"

"I can't say no. I see people like Mark and Elizabeth and they appear to be in love, but my dad doesn't seem to understand that. I certainly don't intend to marry and bring children into the world."

"That's too bad."

"You intend to marry? After what you've been through?"

"I don't know. It depends. But I would like to have a child, to give my love to a child."

"Just think before you do that. It's a total commitment."

"Yes, I know."

"Tell me what you like to do for fun."

"I...I—" Truthfully, she didn't do much for fun. Lately there was only work. "Sometimes I read, watch television. I go to an occasional play if it sounds interesting, or the SMU guest series."

"How about the movies?"

"No, I haven't seen a movie in years. Most of them seem silly."

"A little silly now and then doesn't hurt anything."

"I suppose you're right. So you go to movies a lot?"

"Yeah. I get to hold hands in the movies." He sent her a mock leer.

"You're making fun of me, aren't you?"

"Well, you did get a little bent out of shape about that."

"How would it look if you were taking a woman out on a business luncheon and she insisted on holding your hand?"

"Hmm, you're right, that wouldn't be appropriate. But if it was you, I wouldn't say no."

The waiter delivered their meals, interrupting their conversation, which Diane felt was a good thing. She began eating, keeping her gaze on her plate.

"Is your food good?" he asked.

"Yes, of course, and yours?"

"Perfect, just like my dining companion."

Her eyes shot up, to find him staring at her. "Are you flirting with me?" she demanded.

"Of course I am. Did you just now realize it? I must've lost my touch!"

"I don't find that appropriate behavior at a business lunch."

"I think it depends on whom I'm having lunch with. I never flirt with Mark."

"Good."

"But I'll always flirt with you."

"Why? Don't you respect me?"

"Absolutely, but I also want to sleep with you."

"You're being ridiculous!"

"Did I shock you?"

"Yes. I'm not beautiful. You have all these beautiful women pursuing you. Why would you flirt with me?"

"I'll admit, at first it was because you rejected me."

She rolled her eyes. "I suppose it was the shock of that happening."

He laughed. "Yeah. But then it was because you didn't expect compliments or anything like that. You expected respect."

"And that was so odd? Surely—"

"Most women I know would sell their soul for a rich man. In fact, they usually do. Those are the kind my father marries. I knew instinctively you wouldn't do that."

"That doesn't change the way I look."

"You think that's a problem?"

"Of course. I'm not beautiful. I don't stand out in a crowd."

"You stand out to me. Since I've met you, you occupy my mind most of the time."

She put down her fork and sat back in her chair. "I think you'll get over it quickly."

He gave her a crooked grin, one that touched her heart. "Maybe, but I don't think so."

She picked up her fork and continued eating. What could she say?

After several minutes of silence, he said, "Haven't you thought about me? At least once or twice?"

She thought about not answering, but he'd been honest with her. "Yes, a time or two. But only because you've acted oddly."

"Ah."

She'd hurt his feelings. She knew it, but couldn't help that. She knew she had no chance of a happy ending with someone like John. It would be useless to moon over him.

More time passed, then John spoke again. "If I asked you out to dinner or a movie or something, would you go with me?"

"John, even if I said yes, I don't sleep around. It would only take once or twice going out and you'd be fed up with me. So what's the point?"

"If that happens, then I'll have only myself to blame. Okay? I'm not going to force myself on you. Either we get together because we both want to, or we don't. Those are the rules I play by."

"I suppose I could go out once, but it shouldn't get back to the people at the bank. Do you agree to that?"

"Sure, I can see why that makes sense. I guess I should apologize about wanting to hold hands while we were in the bank. That was bad of me, but I just wanted to touch you so damn bad."

Her gaze collided with his in surprise. "I—I'm not sure—"

"I apologize, Diane. I shouldn't have said that. I'm always in control, I promise."

HE WAS OUT OF CONTROL.

After he left Diane at the bank, John wanted to grind his teeth. He hadn't realized getting her to talk about her life would stir him up so much. She was such a special person, and totally unappreciated by her parents. He'd wanted to pull her into his arms right there in the restaurant.

Which had caused him to be too honest with her.

Then he'd had to retreat and regroup. But tomorrow was Friday and she'd agreed to see a movie with him. First they'd have dinner and then go to the late film.

He'd need to work out at the gym after office hours before he could trust himself to be around her. Looking forward to a date hadn't happened to him since ninth grade. But he'd found a woman who inspired him.

His dad called him that afternoon, but John could hardly keep his mind on the conversation. It kept veering back to Diane.

He'd have to convince her to go out with him again.

He'd have to find something she liked to do, to tempt her the second time. He'd see what was playing at the Dallas Theater Center. Maybe she'd like to go there. Or he could take her to Antares for lunch, up in the Reunion Tower. That was fun, especially if she was afraid of heights. He could hold her against him to keep her safe. He smiled, thinking about the possibilities.

"Son, are you listening to me?"

John brought his attention back to his father. "Sorry, Dad. Say it again."

His dad continued on with his monologue, and John tried to force himself to listen, so he wouldn't be caught off guard again.

Before hanging up, his father said, "By the way, Angi and I want to invite you over for dinner Saturday of next week. Are you free?"

"Yes, but may I bring someone?"

"Oh, you've found someone new?"

"Yes, and I'd like for you to meet her."

"Of course. Who is she? Angi might know her."

"I don't think so. But I'll have to check out the date with her. We haven't been seeing each other much yet."

"Okay, I'll tell Angi to count on two of you for dinner. If she won't come, find another date."

"Right." As if anyone would be interchangeable with Diane. He didn't think so. She was unique.

And somehow that scared John to death.

DIANE FOUND HERSELF in front of her closet again. It really was time to go shopping, for something other than black or gray suits. Luckily she found a casual plum-colored dress in the back.

She hurriedly redid her makeup and wished she'd agreed to go out on Saturday instead Friday, after an entire day at work. But she hadn't thought about that in time. She'd been too swept away when he'd asked her out.

She hadn't intended to accept, of course, but he'd sounded so desperate. That amazed her. No one had ever been desperate to date her. She'd had a steady relationship in college, with a guy who assumed she'd marry him…until he'd fallen in love with another woman.

Diane had been hurt at first, until she realized she really didn't miss him. She just missed having someone. So she kept to herself and finished out the semester. Then she'd gotten a summer job in a bank and found her future. She liked the decorum of a bank, the security. Even changing her studies to fit a career in banking, she had finished her degree early and gotten hired by Guaranty National right after graduation.

She was satisfied with her existence. She didn't have much of a social life, but she'd learned to live without others since she was very young. Diane didn't intend to marry just to have someone around.

But she intended to enjoy the evening, since she'd given in to John's invitation. It wasn't something she'd ever make a habit of, but for tonight, she'd make the best of it.

Diane was just spraying perfume behind her ears when she heard a car out front. She leaned over to look out the window and saw John getting out of his Mercedes, early as usual. She picked up her purse and keys and waited until he knocked on the door.

When he did, joy flooded her, unexpected joy. She didn't think this silly date would mean that much to her. Obviously she needed to get out more often.

She swung open the door, a smile on her lips. But it wasn't John at the door. It was one of her neighbors, a flight attendant who shared the apartment with five of her colleagues.

"Oh, hi, Betsy. How are you?"

"I'm fine, but I was wondering if you could keep an eye out for a package for me. I'm going out tonight and I figured you'd be here." She smiled, as if she hadn't said anything hurtful.

"I'm sorry, Betsy, but I'm going out, too."

"You are? You don't usually—" The woman broke off to stare at the handsome man climbing the stairs. "Damn! Which one of my roommates has a date with *him?*"

Chapter Four

The unexpected swell of satisfaction surprised Diane. She hoped she didn't show that to her neighbor as she quietly said, "*I'm* going out with him, Betsy."

John reached the two women. "You ready, Diane?" he asked.

"Yes, John. I just need to lock my door."

Betsy stuck out her hand as she turned to do so. "Hi, I'm Diane's neighbor, Betsy."

"Nice to meet you, Betsy."

Diane turned around, closely watching John. She wouldn't be surprised to see him checking her out. The statuesque brunette always had boyfriends in and out of the building, but tonight, for the first time ever, she had a date that Betsy wanted. For tonight, at least, Diane could hold her head high. She owed John for that feeling.

Just as she was about to tell him she was ready, the flight attendant handed him a card. "Just in case you're interested," she said, a flirtatious smile on her lips.

Diane had to struggle to keep herself from scratching Betsy's eyes out. But John didn't give her time. He slid his arm around her and moved down the stairs.

When they reached the bottom, Betsy leaned over the railing to say goodbye.

"She's very friendly," John murmured.

"Yes. Maybe you should take *her* out next time." Abruptly, Diane wanted to bite her tongue.

He looked down at her. "You've got to be kidding. She's the same kind of woman my father likes. I have no interest in that type."

It annoyed Diane that relief flowed through her. The man shouldn't matter that much to her. After all, she'd only agreed to a date for one night. And he'd given her a wonderful memory. He and Betsy together.

THEY STOOD IN THE NIGHT air among a crowd of people, looking up at the movie titles on the marquee. His hand rested on her back, where it had been since they'd left dinner. Diane had to admit it felt good, even right in a strange way. With John at her side, she somehow felt different. More feminine.

"Is there something particular you want to see?" John asked. "There's a romantic comedy, an action movie and a western I wouldn't mind seeing."

"A western? You like old-fashioned things?"

"Yeah," he admitted with a grin.

"Me, too. I choose the western."

"I knew you were different from other women."

"Why? What would they choose?"

"The romantic comedy, for sure."

"Not me. I guess I'm kind of an old-fashioned girl. I think I might have been born in the wrong time. Except that I don't want to give up the conveniences and I don't want the limitations put on a woman's choices."

"Then the western it is. I was afraid you were just trying to please me."

"No, I didn't even think about that," she confessed.

He laughed and pulled her into a hug. "You are so good for my ego."

She stepped back from him with a gasp and looked around at the crowd. "John, we're in public!"

"Quit worrying. You're allowed a social life."

"Not with one of my clients!" she snapped, irritated that he would dismiss her concerns.

"So I should have taken you to a cave? Wouldn't you have been suspicious?"

She drew a deep breath and realized what he said was true. "Oh course, you're right."

He put his hand on the small of her back again and escorted her inside the theater. "I hope you saved room for popcorn."

Diane smiled at him. "Absolutely. But I have to say, that was the best steak I've ever eaten." John had taken her back to the restaurant they'd gone that first night, and it totally lived up to its four-star billing.

"I told you. You should've stayed for the meal last time."

Her eyes danced mischievously when she retorted, "Well, unlike this evening, you made that impossible."

He looked sheepish. "I hope you know I've changed my behavior so it won't happen again."

"I'm glad." Even though she kept reminding herself his behavior didn't matter. She'd only agreed to one date. One dinner and a movie. One night.

A night that was racing by way too fast.

WHEN THEY CAME OUT OF THE theater, John still had his arm around Diane, where it had been throughout the whole two hours. He leaned down and asked her, "What did you think of the movie?"

"I enjoyed it a lot. How about you?" She looked up at him to see what he thought.

But John didn't speak. Instead, he stopped walking, bent over and kissed her.

She pulled away, her eyes wide. "You—you shouldn't do that!"

"Why?"

"Anyone could see you! We talked about not letting anyone see us out together!"

"I think you talked about that. I didn't," he said calmly.

Diane didn't know what to say or where to look. She certainly wasn't going to glance up at John. He might kiss her again. She didn't dare let him know how much she'd enjoyed that kiss. After all, it had been several years since a man had taken possession of her that way.

When they reached his car, he opened the door for her and then shut it behind her before heading for his side. That was something else she missed. The special care he gave her every time they went anywhere.

Where had that thought come from? she asked herself. She'd never needed or wanted anyone's care and attention before. Why now? In fact, she'd preferred her independence. She'd managed her life, avoiding anyone who might try to take over her choices.

Right?

Right. And she had to continue, because John had already made it clear what he offered was temporary. She mustn't forget that. Her life was not going to change just because John Davis had a temporary interest in her.

She said nothing on the drive to her apartment, wondering what was going to happen when the date ended. Would he kiss her again? The excitement that seemed to flutter in her stomach worried her. She wanted him to kiss her, she admitted.

Even so, when John pulled into the apartment lot she said, "You don't have to park. I can just hop out."

"No, I always see my dates to the door."

Diane looked at him with mixed feelings, but she didn't protest. After all, no one would see them inside, at her apartment door. And he'd promised he wouldn't force her to do anything she didn't want. All she had to do was be strong.

But it wasn't easy when a big, handsome man had his arms around her and his mouth on hers. She drew a deep breath and got out of the car before he could come open it for her.

John caught up with her and slid his arm around her again. "Are you in a hurry?"

"Uh, no, I just—No, of course not." She felt her cheeks flushing, and hoped he didn't notice.

They walked up the stairs silently. When they reached her door, she turned and offered her hand. "Thank you for a lovely evening."

He took it and carried it to his lips. "Thank *you,* Diane. But this isn't the way I intended to end the evening. I'd rather kiss you good-night."

He was playing dirty pool, making her decide! She squared her shoulders and opened her mouth to deny him the kiss she wanted so badly, but he didn't wait. He wrapped her in his arms again and covered her lips with his.

His were delicious and gave her exquisite pleasure. Maybe more so because she'd been deprived of such intimacy for a long time. She felt like a desert flower after a spring rain. But she mustn't lose control. Even as she thought that, her arms were going around his neck and he was pressing her closer. She knew there was something she should remember, but the sensations that filled her seemed to erase whatever it was.

Until he released her and suggested they go inside.

She jerked her arms down and said, "No! I...I— My apartment is a mess. I can't ask you in tonight."

Obligingly, John stepped back. "Ah, maybe another time, then. By the way, are you busy tomorrow night?"

There was a light in his eyes that made her uneasy. "Why?"

"I have two tickets to the Dallas Theater Center. I thought you might like to go."

"What are they showing?"

"The Producers."

"Oh, I'd love to see it!" she exclaimed. "Are you sure you aren't using the tickets?"

John gave her a sideways grin that tugged at her heart. "Like I said before, my ego certainly won't get too big with you around."

"What did I do?"

"I was asking you to go with me, not offering you both tickets."

"Oh, I'm sorry, I didn't realize—But you said we would just go out once. I'm sure that's what you said." She stepped back and put up her hands. "We're not going to start an affair. That won't work."

"I'm not starting an affair, Diane. I simply have two tickets and it would be a pity to go alone. Won't you come out with me just one more time?"

She knew she shouldn't. But she wanted to see that show. Of course, she could buy her own ticket, but as John said, it would be a shame to go alone. "All right, I'll come."

"Great. We can have dessert afterward."

"You don't have to feed me, John."

"You don't like crème brûlée? They have a terrific one at the Mansion. It has raspberry in it."

Diane's mouth watered and she swallowed before she answered. "Okay, we can go to the Mansion afterward—if you let me pay."

John's eyes narrowed. "I usually pay when I take a woman somewhere."

"But I'm a different kind of woman. You said so yourself. And I don't want you to pay for everything. You bought the tickets, so I buy the crème brûlée."

She thought he wasn't going to agree, and she'd have an out. Not that she really wanted one. The evening sounded wonderful. But at least she wasn't letting him always have his way.

He looked at her a few moments, clearly deliberating. His smile gave away his decision before his response.

Then he leaned down and kissed her again, to seal the deal.

JOHN GOT IN HIS CAR, not bothering to hide his triumphant smile, since Diane couldn't see it. Asking her out on a date took a lot of planning. He knew she'd want to see the show at the Theater Center. He'd had difficulty getting the tickets, but he'd had to find something she wanted to see.

Diane was worth the effort.

Funny how, before meeting her, he'd fallen into the trap of believing his own press. Jonathan Davis, ladies' man. Escort to every socialite and gold digger in Dallas. Connoisseur of beautiful women with great bodies and no brains.

How ironic that with Diane he found her intelligence as attractive as her body.

She challenged him at every turn, and he found himself liking it.

Challenge helped him grow, and gave him more pleasure, too.

Now he had to plan the next date. Maybe dinner with Mark and Elizabeth. Diane would no doubt chastise him for accepting a dinner invitation without her approval, but he thought he could bring her around. He'd call Mark in the morning and set it up for… How soon could he do that? Tomorrow night? No that would be pushing it.

After considering several minutes, he decided on Wednesday night. He didn't want to wait until the next weekend before he saw Diane again.

He whistled the rest of the way home, contemplating the future. It suddenly seemed bright.

INSTEAD OF WORKING at home, Diane went shopping Saturday morning. For the first time in a long time, she had something to shop for other than business suits and somber-colored clothes. She found a number of dresses that looked good on her, showed off the figure that had hidden under her jackets.

Surprisingly, Diane enjoyed seeing her feminine side come out.

She finally bought three outfits, with shoes and a slim purse. After that, she got her hair trimmed and bought a new lipstick for good measure. It was a fun day, one that met a need that had been hidden deep inside of her.

When she climbed the stairs with all her packages, one of the flight attendants, Carolyn, opened the door across from Diane's apartment.

"Oh, I thought maybe you were Marty. She went out an hour ago, and I'm anxious for her to come back."

"No, sorry, I haven't seen her," Diane said, juggling her packages to get to her keys.

"Here, let me help. You've been doing a lot of shopping, haven't you?"

"Not that much." It suddenly occurred to her to invite Carolyn in. "Would you like to see what I bought? I'm a little unsure about what to wear tonight. Do you have time?"

"I'd love to. Shopping is my favorite thing!"

"I'll leave my door open a little so you'll hear Marty when she gets back."

"Thanks, Diane, that's really thoughtful of you."

After they had put the packages down, Carolyn picked up one of the hangers. "This dress is gorgeous."

"I fell in love with it at once." Not that it would fit Carolyn. The tall blond flight attendant had the body of a model. Diane took the other two hangers and laid them over the back of the sofa so she could see them, too. Diane hoped she'd selected fashionable things.

Carolyn nodded to her in approval. "I like both of those, two."

Diane then opened the shoeboxes and brought out the purse she'd bought. "Of course, I can't carry a lot in here, but all I'll need is a lipstick, a comb, my keys and a credit card."

"You should carry a couple of cards in case one of them doesn't work," Carolyn advised.

"Why wouldn't it work?"

"You know, it might be over the limit."

Diane took a moment to consider her answer. Her

card was never over the limit. In fact, she never carried a balance and paid the high interest rates. But rather than explaining that, she simply nodded. Her neighbor was a nice woman, but after a few minutes the discussion of clothes grew tiresome. Diane was glad when Marty arrived and Carolyn went back to the apartment they shared with the other flight attendants.

Diane put away her purchases and then, resisting the laptop that called to her, she took a bubble bath, something she hadn't done in years. She even gave herself a manicure afterward.

Two hours later, she fixed herself a sandwich for dinner and ate while she scanned the New York Stock Exchange reports in the newspaper. It'd been a good week for her clients' investments.

And a good week for her, too. Thanks to John.

She sank back into the sofa. This was terrible. She couldn't keep the man out of her thoughts! But that would change as soon as she wasn't seeing him anymore. And that would occur after this evening, wouldn't it?

She was only going tonight because he'd already gotten the tickets. It would've been rude to turn down such a gracious offer. Besides, she was dying to see that play.

Or was she lying to herself?

The bottom line was she was going to have to be stronger. She'd agree to no more dates after tonight. That had to be her stance. Before she got too used to John's invasion into her life.

Chapter Five

"Don't ever offer me crème brûlée again," Diane sighed as they pulled away from the Mansion in John's car. "It's much too decadent and I have no resistance."

John laughed. "I can see that, judging by the second one you ate."

She clutched her stomach. "Don't remind me. But it was worth every penny."

That it was. He'd loved every minute of watching her enjoy the dessert, and of her reaction to the performance at the theater. Enthusiasm had lit up her face, making her look ten years younger than she usually did in her "banker mode." She was a delight to be with, willingly sharing her insights and enjoyment of the play and the after-theater treat.

All his planning and manipulating had been worth it; he declared the evening wildly successful.

When they reached the fourplex, John again got out of his car and came around to open her door. This time she waited for his assistance. That brought a smile to John's face, and he leaned over to kiss her lips.

"John, why did you do that?"

"To reward you for letting me open your door," he replied matter-of-factly. He put his arm around her waist and she walked silently beside him.

John was mentally preparing his next approach. He knew he'd have to phrase it right, given her resistance. As they started up the stairs, he said casually, "Oh, I almost forgot. Mark and Elizabeth want us to join them for dinner Wednesday night."

Diane came to an abrupt halt at her door. "What? You didn't agree, did you?"

"Well, yeah, I did. Is Wednesday a problem?"

She stared at him, her eyes wide. "I—I can't."

"Why not? I thought you liked Elizabeth."

"Of course I like Elizabeth, but it's a work night."

"So? I promise not to keep you out past ten," he said with his most charming smile.

"No, I work late and do a lot of reading at home. I can't go out during the week."

"What am I going to tell Mark? It's going to look as if you don't like him or his wife."

"Tell him you accepted without checking with me, and I already had plans," she said as she unlocked her door and turned back to face him.

"I can't do that, Diane." He took her hand and gave her a pleading look. "Please, can't you make one exception for me?"

"John, I'm sure Mark will understand."

"I don't think so. He said Elizabeth was looking forward to visiting with you again."

"I don't believe you!"

"Ask Mark. He'll tell you." Fearing rejection, John tried another approach. "What's the big deal? It's just dinner. You have to eat anyway."

"It's just that I—I have a routine that I follow."

"Routine?"

She lowered her head and said in a small voice, "When I get home I usually spend a couple of hours catching up on what I didn't get done in the office, and then I got to bed with some reading."

"Sounds exciting," he deadpanned. "But do you think you can give up all that excitement just for one night?" He kissed her hard and kept his eyes on her.

She looked up at him and he knew he'd won.

"All right, I'll go." Before he got too excited, she added, "But just this once. I can't get involved with you, John. I don't have the time. My work is too demanding and—"

He cut her off with a finger to her lips, silencing her protests. He preferred to revel in his victory. "Thanks for changing your mind," he told her with a smile just before he pulled her into his arms and covered her mouth with his.

In no time he felt lost in her warmth, her womanhood. And he could feel Diane moving with him every step of the way.

When he finally released her, she was breathless. "I…have to go in," she managed to say.

"Me, too," he said with a half smile. "We need some privacy."

She pressed a hand to his chest. "I mean alone, John. I have to go in alone." There was desperation in her voice, almost as if she was trying to convince herself of that.

He moved her hand and nuzzled her neck. "Are you sure?" he whispered.

"Yes, I'm—Stop that!"

"Stop what?"

"Nibbling on my neck."

"You don't like it?" he asked, right before his tongue darted out to taste her skin. She moaned in spite of herself. "Seems as if you do like it."

When she didn't reply, he moved forward, pressing her against her door. "I want you, Diane. Don't you feel it, too?"

She moved back until her spine was plastered against the wood. "No. No, I don't feel that."

"I think you're lying. Your eyes say you want me as much as I want you."

"You're mistaken!" She closed her eyes to prevent him from reading the emotions that she knew were hiding there.

"I think you're lying, sweetheart," he whispered.

"I don't lie. I need to go in now, John. I'll see you Wednesday evening. Where are we meeting them?"

John grinned. "Nice try, honey, but I'll pick you up at six forty-five."

She stiffened and said, "Very well." Then she opened her door and slid inside before he could say anything else.

John shook his head, but as he walked down the stairs he had a smile on his lips.

WHY COULDN'T SHE concentrate?

She reread the numbers on Mrs. Winthrop's portfolio review for the tenth time that morning and still they made no sense. This had never happened to Diane before. Normally she could concentrate through any distractions.

But Jonathan Davis was no ordinary distraction.

Surrendering, she threw down her pencil and walked to the window looking out on downtown Dallas. This was so unlike her, getting all starry-eyed over some man. A man with whom she knew she had no chance, no future. A man who clearly got under her skin and made her unable to do her job.

Why couldn't she shake loose of him?

The ringing phone brought her back to her desk. "Diane Black, Investments."

"Good morning, honey. How are you this morning?"

"Who's calling, please?" she asked, though she knew at once who it was. But she didn't want John to know that.

"It's the guy who kissed you good-night last night. Do you remember now?"

"John, I hope you're in your office with the door closed!"

"Nope. I'm walking through the project we're finishing up. The inspector wanted to see it again."

"Did he hear you?" Diane asked, horrified.

"Sure. That's why I didn't use your name. I know you're shy."

"I am not shy," she practically shouted.

"I hope not, because I'd bet everyone in your department heard that response," he said, and she could hear his grin.

She ignored it. "Where are we going on Wednesday night?" Not even Mark would tell her when she'd asked him first thing that morning.

"It's on a need-to-know basis," John said, "and you don't need to know."

"Yes, I do. I won't come if I don't know the restaurant." She sounded sure of herself, she thought.

"Nope. It's a surprise for you and Elizabeth." Before she could speak again, he added, "I've got to go. The inspector has some questions. I'll see you Wednesday night." He clicked off and just like that was gone.

Diane sat there with the phone to her ear. How was she ever going to work now?

"SHE CALLED, just like you said," Mark said softly into the phone to John. "I told her I was keeping the restaurant a secret from Elizabeth."

"And you told Elizabeth?"

"Yeah. She didn't want to trick Diane, but I told her it was the only way she'd let you drive her."

"Good. I appreciate it, Mark. And I'm looking forward to Wednesday night."

"Yeah, but not because of me and Elizabeth. I know you're using us to bait the trap."

"You know I enjoy visiting with you two. But I'll admit you're the bait this time."

"So what will you use next time?"

"I've got it all set up. I have to go to my father's house Saturday night. I'm going to enlist her to go with me to keep me strong. I think she'll fall for that."

"You're going to fall on your face one of these days, John. Diane's not as dumb as you think she is."

"I've never considered her dumb. But she has a soft heart. I think she'll take pity on me."

"And the time after that?"

"I don't plan that far in advance," John declared.

"I'm not sure I believe that. Just remember, Elizabeth won't forgive you if you upset Diane, and neither will I."

"I haven't lied to her, Mark. And I won't. If she wants to have an affair with me, it will be her choice. I won't force her."

"I know, I know. Okay, I'll see you Wednesday evening."

John hung up the phone; his mood contemplative. He was not lying to Diane. Well, except for the small fib that the invitation had come from Mark. But in the grand scheme of things, that didn't really matter.

All that mattered was how it ended. Him with Diane.

WEDNESDAY. Diane woke up with excitement zinging through her veins, knowing that tonight she would see John again.

She chastised herself for her eagerness. Nevertheless, she counted the hours to dinner.

She knew she wouldn't see or hear from John today. He didn't want her questioning him about the restaurant, or backing out.

Perhaps she was becoming more aware of his behavior. He was being creative, she'd have to admit, but she really couldn't continue to ignore her objections. She was too strong for that. At least she hoped she was.

But he was so sweet to her. Before she got to know him, she would never have used that adjective. But though he put her in difficult positions, he always treated her as if she were a princess. That was addictive, especially for someone with Diane's track record.

An hour later she was well into her day, successfully having pushed John to the back of her mind. When she answered the phone, she almost dropped it when she heard the caller.

"John? Do we need to cancel tonight?"

"Of course not. Why would you think that?"

"I thought you wouldn't call me today."

His low chuckle sent shivers along her skin. "I didn't intend to. But I'd used so much energy not phoning you that I ran out. Have you missed me?"

"Of course not!"

"Not even just a little bit?"

"John, why did you call?" she demanded, hoping to get down to business. It was her only hope.

"I phoned because I miss you. And to tell you I'll pick you up at six forty-five."

"Fine. I'll be ready."

"Would you be ready at six-thirty?"

"Do I need to be?"

"No, but I'd like to show you my latest project. If I pick you up then we'll have time to drive by it."

"I guess we could do that."

"Okay, I'll see you then," he said mildly, as if he'd just been testing her. Then, before he hung up, he said, "I'm looking forward to seeing you tonight."

Probably not as much as she looked forward to seeing him. But instead of voicing that dangerous thought she hung up the phone.

At five o'clock she put all her papers away and locked up her desk. It felt like the middle of the day to someone who normally worked till every other office was vacant and dark. But not today. She picked up her purse and briefcase and headed for the door. Wendy, the receptionist, couldn't hide her surprise.

Diane said good-night and took the first elevator down, hoping she was a little ahead of the general exodus. No doubt her coworkers would wonder about her early departure.

When she got home, she was eager to get ready. After a shower, she sat down to dry her hair. She was wearing it down tonight and wanted it to look good. Half an hour later, she'd done her makeup and her hair, and donned her new heeled strappy sandals and new dress. The flouncy folds of the skirt danced around her legs, making her feel sexy.

How ridiculous to feel so silly about her clothes. But she always wore straight or A-line skirts at the bank. Tonight it felt liberating not to.

She pronounced herself ready, and a minute later the doorbell rang.

Taking a deep breath, she answered it.

John stepped through and, without a single word, took her face between his hands and kissed her like she'd never been kissed before.

Chapter Six

John wasn't surprised when she pulled out of his grasp, but he wasn't happy, either. He'd told himself not to come on so strong, but even the best intentions went up in flames around Diane.

"What's wrong?" he asked her when she backed away from him.

"N-nothing. I—I don't want to mess up my lipstick," she hurriedly said, stepping farther away.

"Then I guess you'd better go add some more, 'cause I've messed it up good." He raised his brows in an exaggerated leer. "Elizabeth is sure to notice."

With a gasp, Diane practically ran from the room.

John wanted to follow her into the bedroom, but he knew such pursuit would be the worst thing he could do. For now.

He simply had to take one step at a time and stick to his plan.

When Diane came back, her lipstick reapplied, she ushered him to the door. "I'm ready. Let's go."

He stepped close and she immediately backed away again. "I'm not going to bite you, Diane."

"Of course not," she said, though her demeanor was still stiff and forbidding. "But I'd like my lipstick to stay in place at least until after I eat."

He grinned. "I can promise that much at least."

Once they were in the car, she said, "I'm looking forward to seeing your new project. Where's it located?"

He gave her the cross streets and began to describe the three-thousand-square-foot luxury condos he intended to build.

After a while, she interrupted him. "Will all of them be deluxe condos? What about more reasonable housing?"

John stared at her. "You think I should build lower priced housing?" he asked in surprise. "You don't make as much profit on lower-priced units."

"That doesn't mean you should ignore that sector of society."

"I realize that, Diane, but this land is special. It requires a special project."

Minutes later he pulled the car to the side of the road beside a several-hundred-acre field with a breathtaking vista of Dallas. "See? People will pay a lot for this view."

"It is a nice piece of property." Nevertheless, she sounded less than convinced.

With a sigh, he said, "Look, Diane, I've built lower- and moderate-income housing before, but the profit margin isn't as high on them…and even you agreed this land is really terrific."

"When's the last time you built inexpensive housing?"

John thought back over his recent projects. And the ones before that...

"Maybe it has been longer than I realized," he admitted.

"THIS HAS BEEN SO MUCH fun," Elizabeth said as she finished eating her entrée. "We should do it on a regular basis."

Both men agreed, but Diane said nothing.

"Didn't you enjoy your meal?" Elizabeth asked her.

"Of course." The Mansion was quickly becoming her favorite restaurant. "But I was thinking about a conversation John and I had on the way here."

Elizabeth's gaze sharpened. "What was it about?"

"His new project." She told her about the land and the housing he intended to build. "I think he should include some moderate housing, too."

Elizabeth looked at her husband and John. "Is that true?"

Mark put his arm around his wife. "Honey, don't worry about it. You make more profit on high-priced properties."

"So you should only build for those who have tons of money?"

"You do if you want to be successful, and John is certainly successful," Mark said with a big grin.

"But what about the people who don't have a lot of money? Like us when we first started looking for a home?"

"Exactly," Diane agreed. "Mixed communities are

more successful. Then you have people who want to work cleaning other people's homes, kids who do baby-sitting jobs and mow lawns. It's a modern community that supports itself."

John stared at her. "I've heard of some communities like that but—"

"You can't change your project now, John," Mark protested.

"I was just thinking out loud, Mark."

"Couldn't he change it if he took the plan to the bank again and got approval?" Elizabeth asked.

"Yes, but he's already got the go-ahead for a great community. He's supposed to start work on it next month."

"I didn't say I was going to change anything, Mark."

"Good. You had me worried there!"

"But it might work on another piece of property I found the other day."

Mark watched him closely. "Just think carefully before you change what you usually do, John. You don't want to make a mistake."

After the waiter came to take their plates away, John sighed.

"What's wrong?" Diane asked.

"I was just thinking about dinner Saturday. It won't be nearly as pleasant."

"Who are you having dinner with?" she inquired, though she chastised herself for caring.

"I have to go to my father's. He and my stepmother invited me to come over. That means they're going to announce the next heir."

"But won't that be exciting?" Diane exclaimed.

"You don't get it, honey. I'm supposed to be happy, but it tells me that their marriage has two years left, at most."

"Did you ever consider you could be wrong this time?"

"I can't think of any reason I'd be wrong. The minute she gets pregnant, she'll expect to be treated like a princess. She won't want to do anything, and will assume everything should be done for her."

"But surely since she's expecting, that's understandable." Diane looked away from John. "I mean, I've never been pregnant, but I'm certain it's difficult."

He took her hand. "Would you come with me? It would help hide my cynicism, which upsets my dad."

"Oh, no, John, it would be a family night and I shouldn't intrude."

"They told me to bring someone, but I couldn't think of anyone, other than you, that I'd want to take. Please, Diane? I'd owe you big time if you'd come. They're not bad people. Dad just never grew up and—and Angi married him for his money."

"John, I don't think—"

This time Elizabeth prodded her. "I can't blame you for not wanting to go, but I believe it is hard on John. I've seen him the next day, and he's always so bitter."

He looked embarrassed, and Diane didn't think he was faking it. What difference would one more evening with him make? "Okay, if you're sure they're expecting you to bring someone, I could go. But I might feel sorry for your stepmother instead of your father."

"Agreed. But I know better." He leaned over and

kissed her cheek. "I really appreciate it, Di. It will make the evening so much more bearable."

She stared at him. "Did you just con me?"

He grinned. "Just a little, but I really need you to go with me. I'd like you to meet my dad, and it isn't an easy evening for me. Especially since my dear stepmother is younger than I am and doesn't hesitate to flirt with me."

Diane stared at him, stunned by his words. "In front of your dad?"

"Yeah. Talk about awkward! The evening seems to last forever."

"I can imagine." She sympathized with his situation, but she also needed to tell him that Saturday night would be the last time she'd go out with him. That's what she'd promised herself. Diane could understand why he needed someone to go with him. But that conversation had to wait till they were alone.

After they said good-night to Mark and Elizabeth and had gotten into John's car, Diane had a question for him. "Why am I the only woman you know you could take to your father's house for dinner?"

"You won't like the answer," he warned.

"What do you mean?"

"I've told you I don't want to marry. Remember?"

"Of course I remember."

"Well, every other woman I know thinks she can talk me into marriage if she just lets me sleep with her. Introducing her to my father would only encourage that assumption. You're the only woman I know who won't think I'm about to propose."

She let out a long breath. That was all too true. She knew she wasn't the marrying kind. Not for John, anyway.

Waiting until he had parked his car at her apartment, she said, "John, I need to tell you something. Saturday night will be our last date."

The smile he'd worn disappeared. "Why do you say that?"

"Because I don't think our dating is a good idea." She hoped that argument convinced him. She didn't have any real reason except for the fear that filled her when he touched her. She knew if she came to count on his warmth, she would be devastated when he left.

"I think it's a great idea. You intrigue me more than any woman I've ever known."

"Only because I didn't fall at your feet or invite you to my bed at once," she retorted. "Once you sleep with me, you won't be interested anymore."

"I bet you're wrong."

"No, I can't risk giving in to you." After saying that she reached for the door handle.

"Wait!" He got out of the car and came around to open it.

"John," she said as she got out, "I've told you there's no need to walk me to the door."

"And I've told you I escort my women home safely."

My women. Diane couldn't admit to the thrill that coursed through her at that label. But she could never be one of John's women, with all that entailed.

When they reached her door, he stepped close to her. "Are you going to invite me in?"

Her hand on his chest kept him an arm's length away. "No. You'd think I was saying yes to…to all you want. I can't risk that."

"What would be so wrong about saying—Damn, don't tell me you're a virgin!"

"No, I'm not a virgin."

He studied her face and she shifted her gaze to the ground.

"How many lovers have you had?"

"How many have *you* had?" she asked in return, lifting her chin in a defiant gesture.

"Enough to be a good lover."

"Me, too, if that's what I want. Now, thanks for dinner." She reached up and kissed him briefly, then unlocked her door before he could protest.

"Come on, Di, that wasn't a real good-night kiss."

"I think it met the definition of a kiss."

He slid his arms around her waist and pulled her forward. Then he covered her lips with his and set her body aflame. When he finally released her, he whispered against her mouth, "Now, *that* was a good-night kiss."

Unable to speak, Diane merely drew a shaky breath and began backing away.

"Where are you going?"

"I—I have to get to sleep. I have to be at work early tomorrow morning."

"Want to meet for breakfast? I know a great place and we can start our day together."

"No, John. Saturday night is it. Now go away!" She

closed the door on his smiling face, wishing she could afford to meet him in the morning. She'd never been invited out for breakfast before. She hadn't spent the night with a man since college, and besides, she was at her desk by eight each morning.

Still, the lingering yearning sounded warning bells in her head. It was a good thing she wasn't going to see him again after Saturday.

She carried her briefcase into the bedroom, got ready for bed and slipped under the covers, prepared to do some work. But her briefcase remained closed beside her, as her thoughts were waylaid by John and his steamy good-night kiss.

She closed her eyes and dreamed of John and his kisses.

"DAD, IT'S JOHN."

"Hi, Son. You're still coming to dinner, aren't you?"

John thought his father sounded a little desperate. Angi must've been in fine form this week. "Yeah, of course, Dad. But I thought I should let you know Diane is coming with me."

"Is she the one you wanted me to meet?"

"Yeah. She's really special."

"I'll look forward to meeting her. Uh, you might warn her that, uh, your stepmother might be a little…you know."

"I know, Dad, and I've warned her. She's okay. She'll understand."

"Good. I'll look forward to seeing the two of you."

"Right. We'll be there."

John hung up the phone, worrying about his dad. Angi must be on a tear. He hadn't heard his dad that concerned in years. Or maybe he was just getting tired of the routine, like John was.

Oh, well, at least it had given him another evening with Diane. He had hoped to talk to her yesterday, but she hadn't answered her phone at work. He'd thought about dropping in to pretend concern about his investments, but he didn't even think he could pull that off.

But, damn it, he really wanted to see her.

Today was Friday. Surely she'd answer her phone tonight. He wouldn't mind a little phone sex, or at least a teasing phone conversation. He just wanted *her*.

It was an interesting feeling. He had no idea how long it would last, but he wasn't seeing any signs of it abating. Maybe Diane was right. Once he slept with her, would he lose his desire for her?.

Not likely.

DIANE'S PHONE RANG. She leaned over and read the caller ID. John again. It was the third time he'd called this evening. But she didn't want to answer. If he was canceling their date for tomorrow night, she didn't want to know. Not tonight, when she was feeling so lonely.

Usually, she kept herself busy, but tonight she was wallowing in misery. It was that kind of night, when she surrendered to the funk. Tomorrow she'd get up and answer the phone when he called. She could deal with his cancellation, if that was his reason for calling.

She hoped not.

She wanted one last night with John. She wasn't falling for him. Of course not. But he'd brought a little excitement into her life. She had to admit she'd gotten in kind of a rut. John had taken care of that.

So why send him away?

That question had been in her head ever since Wednesday night. At first she'd ignored it, but it continued to creep into her mind. And her arguments were growing weaker and weaker.

Would it be so bad? Of course not, until he moved on to another woman. That was the problem with John. There was no happy ever after. There never would be. They wouldn't build a life together, have babies, share triumphs and failures.

They could just sleep together for a while.

And that could be wonderful…until it ended.

She pulled a pillow over her head. This decision was ridiculous.

The phone rang again. Unable to listen to it anymore, she jumped from the bed and picked up the receiver. "Hello?"

"Where have you been?" John barked.

"I've been here."

"I've called and called!"

"You called three times, John. This is the fourth."

"Why didn't you answer?"

She sighed. "I—I was thinking."

"About me?"

"I didn't say that," Diane murmured.

"You're not thinking about canceling tomorrow

night, are you? Because I phoned my dad today, to tell him we were coming."

"I hope he was pleased."

"Yeah. Especially when I told him you'd be under-standing."

"About what?"

"About Angi's behavior. I don't know what she's doing, but Dad sounds pretty fed up. I'm kind of worried about him."

"Maybe he's beginning to recognize the pattern of his own behavior."

"I doubt that. Anyway, we're supposed to be there at seven."

"I remember."

"Good. Now tell me what's bothering you."

"I was thinking about work, John," she lied. "I can tell you about your investments if you have any questions."

"That's not what I mean. Were you really working those three times I called?"

She'd never tell him what—or who—had occupied her thoughts. Instead, she went on the offensive. "Just because I'm going out with you again doesn't mean you have the right to demand to know what I'm thinking about."

"I'd tell you what I was thinking about."

The words tumbled out of her mouth. "I don't want to know!"

He gave a low, sexy laugh. "Coward."

Chapter Seven

Diane stared at the house where John's father lived as they pulled up. It was at least a million dollar home. "Is this where you grew up?" she asked John faintly.

"Yeah. Do you like it?"

"Uh, it's beautiful, but not very homey."

"Yeah, I know, but Dad felt it was important to appear successful. It was my mother's family home originally, and she inherited it. When she died, Dad became owner."

"I think I should've worn a suit. I'm underdressed," Diane said, looking down at the casual outfit she'd chosen.

"Don't be silly. You look great. Dad's going to love you."

She gave him a doubtful look, but got out of the car when he came around to open her door. He took her hand as they walked toward the imposing front door.

"You're sure they're expecting me?" she asked, afraid her nerves were showing.

"If they don't let you in, I won't be joining them," John promised, knowing his father wouldn't betray him.

The door opened and John immediately wrapped the woman who answered in a bear hug.

Diane stood quietly beside him, wondering what was going on. This woman couldn't be Angi....

"Di, this is Mildred, my father's housekeeper. She's the one who raised me after Mom died, in spite of the nannies Dad hired."

"Someone had to take charge of you, John. You were too smart for your own good!" Mildred said with a grin. "Come in, Diane. I'm glad to meet you."

"I'm delighted to meet you, Mildred. I'm sure he was a handful."

The two women exchanged warm smiles. Then Mildred led them into the house. "Your dad is in his office, but Mrs. Davis is in the living room and she wanted to see you first," Mildred whispered.

John frowned. "Is Dad okay?"

"I think so. He's been hanging out in the kitchen, reminiscing a lot."

John's frown deepened, but Diane didn't have time to think about that. They entered a formal living room, a stiff, formal room befitting the millionaire developer, and found Angi, the fifth Mrs. Davis, stretched out on a gold brocade sofa.

She didn't even sit up as they entered. In a languid voice, she said, "Oh, John, it's you. Come kiss your stepmother, darling."

John stopped abruptly, as if surprised by her greeting.

"Angi, allow me to present Diane Black. She's your dinner guest for the night."

"Hello, Diane. Welcome."

"Thank you, Mrs. Davis."

"You can call me Angi. After all, I'm probably younger than you."

Diane wasn't impressed with the woman's manners, but smiled politely.

John turned to her. "Will you be all right with Angi while I go talk to Dad for a minute?"

"Of course." She'd dealt with all kinds of people in her work, and Angi Davis seemed remarkably easy to read.

As he left the room Diane stepped forward and sat down on the sofa opposite Angi's. "It's very nice of you to invite me to dinner, Angi."

"John wouldn't come without you, so I didn't have a choice."

Though taken aback, Diane didn't bother to respond to such a hurtful remark. She leaned forward, picked up a magazine from a nearby table and started thumbing through it.

"Aren't you going to say anything?" Angi demanded petulantly when several moments had passed in silence.

"No, thank you."

"Why are you being so polite? If you want to leave, I'll call a taxi for you."

There was an eagerness in her voice that told Diane that was exactly what she wanted her to do. "It would be rude to leave before John returns."

"I don't think he'd mind. He's very understanding."

With a smile, Diane said, "John wants me here."

Angi snapped to a sitting position before drawing a deep breath. "Don't think he's going to marry you," she said, a hint of amusement in her voice.

Still with a pleasant smile on her face, Diane said, "Really?"

"Really! You probably don't realize it, but he's… interested in someone else."

"No, I didn't," Diane said, her smile still in place.

Angi glared at her. Then, when a sound near the doorway announced John's and his father's arrival, she suddenly covered her face with her hands and burst into fake tears.

Diane looked at John, waiting for his reaction.

"Are you okay, Di?" he asked, coming to her side.

"I'm fine, but Angi seems a little upset."

"Straighten up, Angi," the elder Davis barked. "Mildred's ready to serve dinner."

Diane turned to him, noticing a tired expression on his face. She stood and extended her hand. "Good evening, Mr. Davis. I'm Diane Black."

"I'm glad to meet you. Call me Doug. I was afraid Angi might scare you off while I visited with John."

"She suggested I might have misjudged your son, but I held my ground."

By this time Angi had gotten off the couch. "I don't think I can face dinner!"

"You can take your meal upstairs, if you prefer," her husband stated.

"Don't be silly! I'm the hostess!"

"Then try acting like one," he said sternly. "Come on, Diane. I'll escort you into dinner."

Instead of leaving, Angi hurried over to take John's arm. Diane sent him a sympathetic smile.

Once they were seated at the large table, Doug rang the bell that would bring Mildred with the first course. The housekeeper appeared almost at once with individual salads. Angi was the only one who didn't seem appreciative.

"Mildred, you know I don't care for salad."

Without saying a word, she collected Angi's plate and walked back to the kitchen.

Angi began complaining bitterly, but Doug stopped his wife's ranting. "Mildred is serving my choices this evening, Angi. Deal with it!"

As she again pretended to cry, he engaged Diane in a conversation about her job. When Angi interrupted to say she didn't trust people who invested someone else's money, her husband chastised her, which only brought on more tears, real this time.

Feeling sorry for the woman, Diane asked her a question about the decor of the house. That invoked the resentful comment that her husband wouldn't allow her to change a thing.

Diane looked at John, who shrugged his shoulders. So she tried again, complimenting Angi on her dress sense. That topic was more successful and managed to get them through the salad course.

As a main course, Mildred served sizzling steaks, then offered baked chicken to Angi. Though the younger woman grumbled, she accepted the plate. The entrées were accompanied by a delicious garlic potato dish that Diane loved. She told Mildred that when she came to collect their plates, and the housekeeper beamed.

"Yes, that's Mildred's specialty. I wish her specialty was lasagna," Angi protested.

"Then you'd complain about the calories," Doug said in a bored voice.

His wife had no comeback to that remark, but leaned forward to pick up her iced tea. "I think we should announce our news now, Doug." She turned to John. "You're going to have a new baby brother or sister. If I can carry to term, of course. The doctor says I'm very delicate."

John raised his own glass of tea and said, "Congratulations." Then he turned to his father to discuss a project his dad was working on. Both of them being in the development business gave them common ground, even though they owned and operated separate companies. They'd learned early on that they each worked better on their own.

Feeling sorry for Angi again, Diane said, "That's wonderful news. Congratulations."

"Yes, isn't it? Of course, I'll wear myself out buying a new wardrobe. But it's necessary when you have a reputation as one of the best dressers in Dallas."

"Do you want a boy or a girl?"

"A boy, of course. I don't think a girl would give John a run as favorite son."

"Are his other half siblings all boys?"

"Yes. It seems the Davises only have boys." Her voice took on a challenging note when she added, "Of course, John and I are so close, I won't consider my child to be a half sibling."

"How nice," Diane said. But she didn't try again to keep the conversation going. She was growing too tired of the other woman's petulant manner.

Mildred came in with dishes of baked Alaska, and Diane smiled in delight. "Oh, I love this dessert."

In a studied drawl, Angi said, "Mildred does an okay job. But I've had better."

"Don't eat yours if you don't like it, Angi," Doug suggested.

She drew her dessert plate closer and shot him a furious look.

After dinner, Angi announced that, due to her delicate condition, she was going to bed early. To Diane's surprise, she bade her goodbye and politely thanked her for coming. Then she ran to John, catching him off guard as she flung her arms around his neck.

He caught Angi by her waist, clearly trying to put some distance between them.

"Did you want to check if I still have my slim figure?" she asked coyly.

"No, Angi. I wanted to keep you from plastering yourself all over me. Good night."

She pouted. "I thought you'd give me a congratulatory kiss, at least."

"I certainly congratulate you on your good news, but that's all you're getting."

With tears in her eyes, she turned and ran out of the room. Doug stood there staring after her. Then he turned back to his son. "She's crazy about you, you know."

"She just wants whatever she can't have."

"True. Well, let's go in the den so we can be comfortable."

The room was in direct contrast to the living room. Here Diane felt at home as she settled on a comfortable tweed sofa. John immediately sat down beside her and took her hand in his.

Doug stared at their clasped hands and then at his son. "I see why you said she'd understand. Diane, I apologize for anything my wife may have said."

"It's all right, Doug. Don't worry."

He sighed and visibly relaxed. "Thank you. I hated to take John aside before Angi had settled down, but I needed to get some things cleared up."

"Dad—" John began, and Diane could feel him tensing up.

"No, Son, I don't want to talk about it. Tell me about Diane. When did you two meet?"

"When I was trying to make you happy."

"What? What's he talking about, Diane?"

"He came to meet Jennifer Carpenter, and mistook me for her."

"I assumed she was Jennifer because she answered her door," John explained.

"Where was Jennifer?"

"On her honeymoon." John grinned. "I was a little late doing what you asked."

"I guess so, but it turned out well for you."

"Not at first, but I've worked my way into Diane's heart!"

She said nothing, even when Doug gave her a questioning glance.

John immediately asked, "Why are you looking at her? Don't you believe me?"

"Of course I do—as long as the lady doesn't say different," Doug stated, with a grin remarkably like his son's.

John carried Diane's hand to his lips. "She wouldn't lie to you."

"Well, I guess that proves one thing."

"What, Dad?"

"That you should've taken my advice in the first place. I knew what you needed."

"If I'd taken it when you told me to, I would've met Jennifer, not Diane."

"So we were both right!"

"Maybe," John said. Then he stood and pulled Diane up with him. "We'd better be on our way, but don't worry about the other. I'll take care of things if…if it becomes necessary."

"I know, boy. I just wanted to be sure."

John hugged his dad and Diane shook his hand. "Thank you for inviting me to dinner."

Doug leaned over and kissed her cheek. "I'm so glad you accepted. You're perfect for my boy."

Once they were in John's car heading back to her apartment, Diane said, "Is your dad all right?"

"According to him, his doctor said he needs to slow down. Not that he can, with Angi at his heels." John shook his head in disgust. "Tell me, how nasty was my dear stepmother after I left the room?"

Diane chuckled. "She let me know you weren't the settling down type, which you'd already said."

"She didn't!"

"Does it matter? It was easy to see why she wanted to get rid of me. You showing interest in me made her desperate. I think, in her mixed-up mind, she wanted to tie you to her before she lost her figure. I assume doing so is a major catastrophe for her?"

"Yeah. I didn't think she'd even want a baby, but I gather my dad had already been losing interest. Her tantrums must've worn him down."

"I can understand that."

"Me, too. I think Dad would be better off if he'd separate from her now. He'd definitely lead a more peaceful life. Angi fights with Mildred a lot."

"Probably because she feels Mildred has more power than her," Diane speculated.

"Yeah."

He sounded glum, and Diane understood. His father wasn't doing well, and there wasn't anything John could do.

For his sake, she prayed his father lived a long life. It had been nice to see the obvious warmth between the two men.

When they reached Diane's apartment building, John walked her upstairs to her door.

Diane already knew what she was going to do, she'd made the decision last night.

When she unlocked the door, John kissed her lightly and said, "Good night, Diane. Thanks for coming."

"Don't you want to come in?" she murmured.

He froze for a moment. Then he asked, "Are you saying what I think you're saying?"

"Yes."

He bent to kiss her, then lifted his head, his gaze burning. "I promise you won't be sorry, Di."

"No, I won't."

Even though the time would come when he would leave her, she'd decided she wouldn't be sorry. She'd have him in her life for a while. She had never planned on marrying anyone, anyway, so she'd simply enjoy their time together.

When they entered her apartment, John sat down on her couch. "Why don't you pack a bag? I can wait."

She stared at him. "Why would I pack a bag?"

"So we can go back to my house."

"No, thank you. If you want to make love, we'll do it here. If not, you can go home now."

"Man, you are one stubborn woman." He stood and shrugged off his suit coat. Then he untied his tie. Laying both on the back of the sofa, he said, "Shall I strip naked right here?"

She hid her smile. He was trying to get a rise out of her, but she was going to stay calm. "In the bedroom, please."

She entered first, knowing she'd left the room perfectly neat in case she brought John in. She gestured to the bathroom. "Would you like to disrobe in there?"

"Sure. Whatever you want."

After he went into the bathroom, Diane undressed and put on a silk robe. She was turning down the bed as she heard the bathroom door open.

John stood there with a towel wrapped around his waist. His chest was broad, as were his shoulders, and muscles rippled in his arms. She sucked in her breath.

Stalking across the carpet in his bare feet, he reached her and put his arms around her. "I'm so ready for this, honey. I've been making love to you each night, only you weren't there. I can't wait to hold you for real." Then he kissed her, a deep, passionate kiss that almost took her breath away. She collapsed against his shoulder when he released her.

"What are you wearing?" he asked.

"A robe, of course."

"I want you to take it off. Here, I'll help," he added as her hands went to the belt. "Do you have anything on underneath?"

"No. I didn't think you'd like that."

"You're right," he said as he opened the knot and parted the robe. It was his turn to draw in a breath. Then he scooped her up into his arms and laid her on the white sheets. "You are incredibly beautiful. Even better than I dreamed."

She couldn't believe she was hearing those words, or that she was here with John, in her apartment, in her bed. But it was real and she wouldn't forget a single minute of it. "You're still wearing my towel." She smiled coquettishly at him.

"I can take care of that," he whispered as he released it.

He stood there in full arousal. "I think I may need to catch up a little," she said, more breathlessly than she'd wanted to sound.

"No problem. I'm going to help you." He joined her on the bed and cupped her breasts in his large hands. "You are so beautiful, Diane." His mouth joined his hands and a jolt of desire coursed through her, unlike anything she'd experienced before. She pulled him closer and their lips met again and again. While they kissed, his hands explored her body. She did the same, letting her fingers slide over his muscled arms, his broad chest, flat stomach. And even lower.

True to his word, as always, John brought her to the brink of climax. When he nudged her for entry, she was more than ready, opening her legs for him. Hungry, she took all of him in. Heat suffused her, burning up all conscious thought but one.

Why had she waited so long?

JOHN WAS OVERWHELMED BY the passion that drove him. When they'd both enjoyed the release their lovemaking brought, he whispered, "Di, are you all right? I didn't hurt you, did I?"

In a slurred, slow voice, she said, "No. You were— incredible."

Her head was on his shoulder and she seemed to be asleep. But she said one more thing. "Lock the front door when you leave."

John raised up and stared at her. She expected him to leave? Not likely. "Yeah, later," he whispered. Then he gathered her in his arms and held her, warm and soft, against him. It was as if they'd been made for each other. She fit perfectly against him. He hoped she slept late in the morning. He wanted all the time he could get with her in his arms.

Chapter Eight

When Diane woke up the next morning, she was alone.

As she'd planned, she reminded herself. But John's lovemaking had been so exquisite, she hoped he wouldn't break off with her after just one night.

Then she chided herself for that thought. She knew she couldn't hold him. She probably didn't have enough experience to interest him.

Her dreamy, half-awake state was shattered by the sound of the bathroom door opening.

She sat upright in bed. "I thought you'd gone!"

"How could I when you offer such a beautiful sight to tempt me?" John asked, staring at her bare breasts.

She shrieked and yanked the sheet over her.

"Di, why are you covering up? We made love last night. I think I memorized every curve of your body."

"I'm not used to appearing naked in front of anyone," she said, still with the covers pulled up. He sat down on the bed and tugged the sheet out of her hands. "You have the softest, sweetest breasts I've ever seen," he whispered, just before he kissed her.

She wanted to tell him he had the most seductive lips, but she didn't. She was too busy kissing him back.

He was fully aroused in no time and she found herself letting him—no, encouraging him to—make love to her again.

This time, when they reluctantly drew apart, Diane didn't fall asleep. She traced the vee of hair on his chest down to his stomach. He grabbed her hand when he thought she'd gone far enough.

"It will take me a little while to recover, sweetheart," he whispered.

"I didn't mean—I was just fascinated by the way— I'm not used to being around a naked man, either."

"And I don't want you getting used to anyone else's body," he said with a kiss. "How about I run home and shower and change. Then I'll come take you out to breakfast."

"I'd like that," she said, dying to ask him if he was still going to see her after today. But she supposed she'd know soon enough if he didn't come to her door again after today.

THOUGH SHE HAD a hot shower herself, Diane's body ached from her activities with John. And her hunger seemed to have quadrupled. John took her to a pancake house, and she ate every forkful of a stack of hotcakes.

"So, making love makes you hungry?" he asked with a leer.

"John, shh!" she ordered in a stage whisper. "You don't have to announce it to the world."

"I'd like to," he assured her, "but I won't because I don't want to embarrass you."

"I appreciate it."

After he paid for their breakfast, he looked at Diane. "So, what do you want to do for the rest of the day?"

"Don't you have plans?"

"Nope. I'm at your service."

Her Sundays usually consisted of work, laundry and reading the paper. But not today. Today she would put herself in John's hands. "What'd you have in mind?"

"I thought maybe I'd go through the Parade of Homes. You interested?"

The Parade of Homes was an exhibit of new houses decorated by prominent and up-and-coming interior designers. Diane was game, but wondered why John was. She asked him.

"I go every year, looking for new talent to decorate my model homes when I build them," he replied, leading her to the car. "Plus I appreciate the architecture."

That he did, Diane realized later as they wandered through the homes. He made notes and commented on several unique features, and she found they had similar tastes in interior design. When they finished, their late breakfast had been worked off, and they were both hungry again.

"I know the perfect place for lunch," he said as she rejoined him after visiting the restroom.

"Where? Most restaurants will have stopped serving."

"Not this place," he said. "Trust me."

After a short car ride, Diane looked up to find herself in the same neighborhood where John's father lived, but the house he parked in front of was quite different. It was a relatively new one, modern, with great curb appeal.

"Where are we?"

"We're having lunch here."

"But, John, I can't meet someone now. I'm all wind-blown and have no makeup on!"

"You look beautiful as always, Di. Come on, you'll be fine." After he helped her out of the car, he took her hand and they walked up to the front door. It reminded her of last night, when they'd arrived at his dad's. But this time he didn't ring the doorbell; he walked right in.

"John, what—"

"You're right on time, Mr. Davis. And this must be Miss Black. Welcome, ma'am." The woman greeting them was younger than Mildred, but Diane finally figured out where she was. In the entryway of John's home.

"I hope John gave you warning," she told the woman.

"Of course I did," he said. "This is my housekeeper, Mrs. Walker."

"I'm delighted to meet you, Miss Black."

"Same here. Please, call me Diane."

"I will if you call me Gladys."

"Gee, she never asked me to call her by her first name," John said with a smile.

"Well, of course you can, Mr. Davis," Gladys said.

"Only if you call me John."

"Of course," she agreed, her cheeks red. "Lunch is ready, if you'll just come this way."

She led them to a small room next to the kitchen.

"John asked that I serve you here, because the dining room is rather large. He takes most of his meals in here."

"I can see why. It's charming."

"Thank you," John interjected. "I think so, too."

He asked Gladys to join them, and the three of them enjoyed their lunch, discussing several topics, including the tour of homes. John mentioned that he had a lot of the details in his home that Diane had liked. When they'd finished eating, he asked, "Would you like a tour?"

"I should help Gladys with the dishes—" Diane began, but the housekeeper cut her off.

"You go along. It will give me time to put the kitchen straight. I know you'll like the house."

John gave Diane a thorough tour of the professionally designed home. It had four bedrooms, a private office, living room, dining room, den and five baths, in addition to a covered patio beside a kidney-shaped swimming pool, where they ended their tour.

"You really have a palace here, don't you?" Diane teased.

"No, it's not ridiculously overdone, like some of those houses we saw today."

"I agree. Your house is so much more a home."

He bent down and kissed her. "I'm glad you like it."

"I do. Now I need to tell Gladys goodbye and head home. I have to get ready for work tomorrow."

"Okay. You go talk to Gladys. I'll be back in a second."

Diane found the kitchen spotless as she entered, and Gladys just sitting down with a cup of coffee.

"Oh, come in, Diane. Would you like some coffee?"

"I'd love one, thank you. This house is gorgeous. You must work yourself to death keeping it so sparkling clean."

She smiled, her blue eyes twinkling. "No, I really have a cushy job. With only Mr.—I mean John, living here, there's not that much to do. And once a week a cleaning service comes in to do the vacuuming and the baths."

"I'm glad to hear it. I don't think one person should have to clean such a big house."

"I keep thinking maybe John will marry and have a family. He has plenty of room here. It would be nice to see him settle down."

Hiding a frown behind her cup, Diane said, "I don't think that's in his plans."

"What plans?" John asked as he entered the kitchen, carrying several hangers with items of clothing over his shoulder.

"Uh, plans for a family," Diane said. "What are those?"

"Some of my clothes. Ready to go?"

"Yes, of course. I'm glad I got to meet you, Gladys, and thanks for such a lovely lunch."

"Anytime, Diane."

After they got in the car, she asked, "Are you going by your cleaners today? Are they open on Sunday?"

"No, but I can go by tomorrow."

"But you'll be back home before then."

"I will? Are you throwing me out tonight?"

Diane turned to stare at him. "What?"

"I asked if you were throwing me out this evening? I'd like to spend the night again. Is that a problem?"

"Uh, no. But I need to get ready for work."

"What does that entail?"

"I have to do my nails, some laundry, catch up on some work…. Then I relax and watch my favorite TV show."

"You don't have to entertain me, Di. I'll manage on my own."

"But I don't have anything for dinner."

"So, I'll go out and pick up a pizza. You like pizza, don't you?"

"Yes," she said slowly, still trying to think. She'd figured he might take her out a few times on the weekends and that would be the end of their "relationship." It appeared John had a different idea.

"Good."

"John," Diane said, swallowing convulsively, "is this why you tire of the women you've gone out with? You date them nonstop and then change people the next weekend?"

"No, it's not. Usually I date a woman once a week, waiting to find out if I want to keep seeing her. Which I usually don't. But you are something different. I can't find a time I *don't* want to be with you. If you get tired of me, you'll have to kick me out. Deal?"

"Deal," Diane agreed, smiling slightly. Somehow she didn't think she would be the one walking away.

Once they were inside her apartment, he asked, "Mind if I hang these in your closet? They won't take up much space."

She gestured toward her bedroom. "Go ahead." Then she stood in the middle of the living room, suddenly feeling awkward in her own place.

He came back out and tugged her against him for a kiss that she tried to resist.

"What's wrong?"

"If I let you distract me, I won't get anything done."

He pulled his hands back. "Go get busy."

But as she turned to head into the bedroom, he patted her on her backside, surprising her.

"What are you doing?" Diane yelped.

"Just giving you a little love pat." He kissed her again. "Now, quit taking up my time. Go!"

Diane couldn't help laughing. His teasing made her heart feel lighter as she tackled her chores.

A couple of hours later, during which she had washed a load of clothes, given herself a manicure and caught up on some work, John knocked on her bedroom door. When she called out, he opened it.

"I'm going to go get us a pizza. What do you like?"

"Green peppers, lots of cheese."

"Okay. I can live with that," he assured her. He turned away, then swiveled back and said, "If you'll give me your key, I can make me a copy of it while I'm out."

She stared at him. "Why?"

"In case I get home from work before you do. Do you want me standing outside your door until you get home?"

He wanted a key? He wanted to see her on a week-night? Diane wondered if he was playing a joke on her. But it made sense, didn't it? In a pushy kind of way. "Okay, here's my key," she said, reaching for her key ring. "I just didn't think—Well, whatever you think."

She stood very still as she heard him go out. One of

the flight attendants from next door must've been coming up the stairs. He greeted her without stopping.

Wasn't he even attracted to her neighbors? All six flight attendants were beautiful women. But Diane didn't think he even stopped to introduce himself.

At the knock on her door she hurried to open it, thinking John had changed his mind. She swung it open, only to find her neighbor Carolyn, the blonde with the model body.

"Who is that gorgeous hunk who just left your apartment?" she gushed. "Is he a brother or a friend or what?"

Diane realized all the choices were staid and safe. Obviously, the woman didn't think Diane could attract a man like John. "He's my lover."

Carolyn's jaw dropped. "You're kidding."

"No, I'm not. Didn't he introduce himself?"

"No, he just said hi and kept going. He's your *lover?*"

"Yes. Why do you doubt me?"

"You just…well, you've never seemed interested in dating. And he—he, Diane, seems like the type to be interested in!"

"I agree," Diane said, moving back to close the door.

"How about I come over and ask him to a party? That'd be okay, wouldn't it?"

"Certainly!" Diane snapped as she shut it. Then she banged her head against the wooden panel. She shouldn't have agreed to such a stupid thing. John might think she didn't want him here with her. Maybe if she explained—

The sound of a car door closing had her spinning around, running into the bedroom to peer out the window. No, John's Mercedes wasn't there. She drew a deep breath. What was wrong with her? She couldn't spend the whole time he was gone running to the window every time a car pulled into the lot.

She would go into the living room and find something to do. And she did, until she heard the key in the lock and her door opening.

"John, I'm so glad you're back!"

He laughed. "I like that greeting. I'll go out and come in again. It's worth a second trip."

"No! I have to explain! I didn't mean to—She wanted to know if you—I didn't know what to say—"

John walked over and wrapped his arms around her. "Calm down, honey."

"I just didn't want you to think I—"

He kissed her.

They broke apart when they heard a knock on the door.

"Here," he said, picking up the pizza box. "Put it in the kitchen. We'll eat as soon as I get rid of this." He nodded toward the door, then walked over and opened it.

Diane took one look at Carolyn in a sexy dress and ran for the kitchen.

"HELLO," Carolyn said with a siren smile. "I'm a next-door neighbor of Diane's. I wondered if you'd like to come to a party."

"Well, that's very nice of you, but Diane and I—"

"Oh, she's not invited! I mean, Diane never comes to our parties," she said, recovering her smile.

"Then I don't think I will, either. But thanks for asking." He closed the door, even though Carolyn was still standing there. It was satisfying, turning the lock. Had the woman hurt Diane? Surely she didn't think he'd go anywhere without her.

Somewhat tentatively, Diane walked into the living room, two plates of pizza in her hands. "What did you say to Carolyn?"

"I said I wasn't interested in her party."

"You did?" A smile replaced the uncertain expression on Diane's face.

"I did. I told her I only went places with you. I hope you don't have a problem with that."

"I don't. I like it."

"Good. Then let's eat."

He took the plates from her and strode toward the sofa. She'd had the television on and his favorite show, a police drama, began. He patted the cushion next to him. "Sit here," he said, "right next to me."

He slipped his arm around her and they ate in companionable silence. Enjoying the food, the company and the program.

Till it ended and John dropped a bomb.

"Let's take a shower together."

Chapter Nine

Diane could only stare at him. "What did you say?"

"I said we should go take a shower together."

"Why?"

"I just thought it would be fun. You still seem a little nervous about being naked with me. Why not?"

"Well, my shower's not that big. I'm not sure we could get really clean."

"Honey, I'm not interested in getting clean. I'm interested in fulfilling a fantasy."

Diane gasped.

When the oxygen flowed once again to her brain, she realized the idea had appeal. She just needed to warm up to it.

After all, her one affair had been in college, and they'd only had her boyfriend's car. It had been dark and cramped, with no room to enjoy each other. It hadn't even been much fun. She hadn't realized that until now. With John, sex was something to revel in.

"I'd love to!" she suddenly exclaimed.

He looked down at her. "Are you sure?"

"Yes, I'm certain. I want to enjoy what we're doing. I've never done that before."

"Honey, I'll take you any way I can get you. But I think you'll enjoy a shower. Come on."

He led her into her bathroom and helped her undress, teasing her about her manicure and pedicure, helping her feel at ease. Then he turned on the water.

She actually had a large shower, and once they were inside, she realized this was an opportunity to become acquainted with his body as much as he was learning hers.

They spent a half hour under the spray, soaping each other, stroking and exploring. Diane found the feel of John's body covered with feminine soap bubbles strangely arousing. The hard muscle under the slippery soap stirred her senses. They continued until John called a halt.

"Come on, let's go to bed."

She had no argument there. They dried off, which was almost as much fun as the shower, and ran for the bed. In no time they were in the throes of lovemaking.

After they relaxed again, she lay in his arms and whispered, "I don't think I'll ever think of a shower the same way." Her limbs seemed to weigh a ton, and she could barely keep her eyes open.

"Honey, have you got everything done you needed to do?" he whispered.

She had no idea what he was asking, but she said yes. It was the most conversation she could come up with.

"Then go to sleep. I'll get us up in time tomorrow morning."

She didn't hesitate to float off in his arms.

JOHN CUDDLED DIANE against him, thinking about their activities that night. She had seemed so surprised that they weren't in the shower just to get clean, but to pleasure each other. They'd done both, and had built on their intimacy.

She seemed to expect him to walk out at any moment.

Well, maybe he deserved that, but he wasn't ready to leave her. He didn't know when he would be ready. She was so strong, so lovable, so…

Of course, they would probably part at some point, but he didn't want to think about that now. He wanted to enjoy the time he had with her.

He set the alarm before he went to sleep. Making her late to work would be a mark against him. He had to prove to her that he could make her life better, not worse. That was his goal.

DIANE WAS NERVOUS about their first morning together on a workday. Would John want to shower together again? Her morning routine was regimented down to the minute to get her to work early. There'd be no room for dalliances like that. Nor matter how enticing.

She needn't have worried. John had got up and taken his shower before she woke. He was already in the kitchen making breakfast.

"I don't eat much breakfast," she said, to be polite. The truth of the matter was she never ate breakfast on a weekday.

"Haven't you heard it's the most important meal of the day? Now get in the shower," he ordered.

After they ate the scrambled eggs and toast John had cooked, they took turns in the bathroom to shave and do makeup. It worked amazingly well, considering they'd never gotten ready together before.

"All set to go?" he asked.

Today he didn't have any meetings, so he was dressed in jeans and a golf shirt, looking sporty and casual. Diane was dressed in one of her suits, her makeup subdued, her hair pinned up in a French braid.

But somehow, they matched. She was smiling at him and he couldn't resist snatching a kiss.

"Did I mess up your lipstick?"

"No. I'm learning. I have some in my purse. I'll reapply it when I get to work."

"In that case…" He kissed her again. And again at her car.

"I can't wait to see you tonight."

She gave him a worried look. "I'm not usually home till late."

"Come home early and I'll make it worth your while." He pulled her close and her body instantly reacted. "I'll get here early, so I may go grocery shopping for some things I like to have."

"Just make me a list and I'll go shopping tonight, after I get home."

"We'll work it out, honey. I don't want to make your life harder."

John kissed Diane goodbye and watched as she got in her car. He suddenly didn't want her out of his sight. What if something happened and she needed him?

He almost ran after her, to warn her to be careful, but he held back. He didn't want her to know how needy *he'd* suddenly become.

ALL DAY LONG Diane couldn't get John's comments out of her mind. *Come home early and I'll make it worth your while.* Just the thought of what awaited her spurred her to work faster and more efficiently so she could get home to him.

"Are you in a hurry tonight?" Wendy asked her late in the day.

Was she that obvious? she thought. "Y-yes, I need to do some grocery shopping tonight. That messes up my routine, but I didn't get it done this weekend."

"You were busy on the weekend?"

Diane didn't take offense at the surprise in Wendy's voice. "As a matter of fact, yes, I was."

Luckily, Wendy didn't ask with whom.

A phone call from one of her largest clients just before closing threw her schedule completely off. He'd heard a rumor of a corporate takeover that, if true, would cause his investments to nosedive. Diane tried to calm him down, but he seemed to grow more hysterical by the minute. She anxiously looked at her watch, worrying about John, which shocked her when she realized what she was doing. Her work was more important, wasn't it?

Trying to reassure the man, she promised to do some research and call him back. Then she began to phone contacts who might have some information. When she finally tracked down the rumor and realized it was untrue, she called her client back, able to satisfy him that his fortune was still safe.

It was almost seven when she finally got home. John wasn't there.

The silence echoed.

This was ridiculous. How had she let this man turn her around so quickly? She used to like her life, her quiet, regimented, solitary existence. But suddenly, with John in her world, she looked forward to her days…and especially her nights. And not for work.

She put down her briefcase and wandered into her bedroom to change.

Next, she took stock of her pantry and refrigerator. It was a wonder John had even found eggs and bread that morning. She'd really let things slip since he'd come into her life.

Making a list as she went through everything, she was just about to head out to the grocery store when she heard a key in the lock.

She immediately ran to the door, hoping he hadn't come to tell her goodbye. When he pushed it open, she saw he had bags of groceries in his hands.

"You went grocery shopping already? I was just getting ready—"

He bent over and kissed her. "That's the best I can do until I put these groceries down."

She followed him to the kitchen, where he set the bags on the counter, then turned and hugged her to him, covering her lips with his.

"Mmm, I've missed that all day long," he said with a grin.

So had she. More than she cared to admit.

When he turned to start unpacking the sacks, she hurriedly offered, "I can do that."

"Okay. I'll go get the other bags."

More food? For whom had he been shopping? Diane began unloading the paper bags and found he'd bought things she'd never splurge on. Like thick sirloin steaks and a whole barbecued chicken. She didn't eat that much.

He entered with two more sacks.

"You spent a lot of money. Tell me how much and I'll reimburse you," she said at once.

"No way. These are my groceries. You can buy your own."

"Oh, so you're not going to share those steaks or any of that barbecued chicken? I know you have a bigger appetite than me, but I didn't think it was that big."

He grinned. "I might share…if you're good." Together they finished storing the groceries and he then took her in his arms again. "Now, let's go out for a quick dinner."

"After you bought all that?"

"Why not? We'll cook those things later in the week. Tonight we're already tired."

"I think I should cook, since you did the shopping. I'm sorry I was so late." Truthfully, though, she was never home by seven. Not before she'd met John.

"You can tell me about your day over dinner. Come on. Let's go find some food."

They enjoyed a quick meal at a nearby restaurant. Afterward, John reminded her he'd bought ice cream for dessert.

"I saw that, and it happens to be my favorite flavor."

"You like Cookies and Cream, too? That's great!" John beamed at her.

"You're easy to please."

"See if you say that later," he teased with a mischievous gleam in his eye.

They hurried home then. But they never made it to the ice cream.

SEVERAL TIMES in the next month, they went out to dinner with Elizabeth and Mark, enjoying their companionship. They even went out with a couple of other friends John wanted Diane to meet.

She found the wives of John's other friends were more like Angi than Elizabeth. There was a streak of pettiness and jealousy in those women, but Diane tried not to let it bother her. After all, he was going home with her.

They also returned to John's house for dinner at least one night a week. He said he had to keep in touch with Gladys, who, at their invitation, always joined them for dinner. It gave John a chance to catch up on what was going on in the neighborhood.

Diane's life was expanding so much, even without the many romantic moments she shared with John. For the first time ever, she shared every intimate detail with another person.

John complimented her at every turn and supported her in anything she wanted to do. Having never had parents who backed her, she found his support unbelievable.

Trying to return the favor, she worked hard to believe in his projects and take an interest in them. She felt it was the least she could do.

One evening, John brought up her idea about a project with multiple levels of housing. She looked up but didn't offer any comment.

"Have you changed your mind?" he asked.

"No, I haven't, but that's your business."

"Well, I think I've decided to do as you suggested. I acquired some land I've been looking at, and I think it will be a perfect location. It has good bus routes on the exterior, good for lower priced housing, and I can put more expensive housing toward the inside."

"I like that idea."

"Good. I've got some house plans, but I want you to look at them and tell me what you think."

Diane enjoyed sharing her opinions, enjoyed the healthy give-and-take in their relationship. John valued her feelings and put them above all else.

As they approached Thanksgiving, he warned her one night at dinner that he'd promised his dad they would join him and Angi for dinner. "Is that okay with you?"

"I'll manage."

"You could invite your parents," John suggested casually.

Diane's head snapped up and she stared at him across the table. Then she looked away. "No. Thank you, though."

"Why not?"

"My parents and I don't socialize." She continued to avoid his gaze.

"But, honey, maybe they'd be interested in what you do."

She shook her head and didn't bother to give excuses.

"Okay. But they'd be welcome."

"No, they wouldn't. Not by me."

"We could ask them out to dinner some evening, just the two of us."

"No, John. Leave the subject of my parents alone."

"Okay. Did Jennifer get back from her honeymoon?"

"Yes. I talked to her when they returned, but they've bought a house and they're moving out."

"Will you miss her?"

"Yes, she's a good friend. We'll invite them to dinner some evening."

"With their three children?" John asked in alarm.

"We could ask them to come alone. Once they get settled in their new home."

"Good. I don't know how to make conversation with kids."

"It's not that hard, John," Diane protested.

"You want me to give up on your parents, and I will. But you have to give up on me and kids. Okay?"

"Okay," she agreed quietly. She had no choice. She'd gotten to the point that she didn't think she could live without John. Though she still warned herself the day would come when he would leave her, she dreaded it desperately.

But she would have wonderful memories. Of their lovemaking, the sharing of their daily lives, doing little chores together. Everything seemed so much more fun with John by her side.

Even her work was going well. She'd found a stock she'd believed in, and had invested several of her clients' funds in it, including John's and Mrs. Winthrop's. It had suddenly shot up beyond her wildest dreams. When the steep rise started leveling off, she pulled Mrs. Winthrop out and invested her profits in a safer stock, but asked John what he wanted her to do.

"What would you do if it was your money?" he inquired.

"I still believe in the stock and I'm staying in it for the time being."

"Then, honey, let mine ride, too. I trust you."

"But, John, I could be wrong."

"I know." He bent and kissed her. "But it's a risk I'm willing to take." She knew all about risks. She was taking one with her heart.

Diane still kept their relationship a secret in the financial community. It wouldn't be to her advantage to let people know about her and John.

But she wasn't ashamed of what she was doing. John had liberated her from a lot of the rules she had followed, all her life, many of them for no reason. And she'd never been happier.

The next evening they had dinner at John's house.

"I'm so glad you let me cook for you once a week," Gladys said as she served them a delicious-looking roast. "Otherwise I'd be doing nothing to earn my salary. Diane, don't you want to live here, instead of your apartment?"

"I'm warming to the idea slowly, Gladys. We've only been together for six weeks," she pointed out, and then shivered suddenly.

"What's wrong, honey?" John asked.

"I don't know. It was like I was jinxing us. What if we don't last much longer? Then I would've moved for nothing. It's not like I own my place, Gladys. I just need some time."

"Or someone to ask you to make it permanent," the woman said, staring at John.

"What are you looking at me for? We're doing just fine the way things are. And I'm getting my money's worth from you," he told his housekeeper. "You take my messages and keep my house in good shape."

"Whatever you say," Gladys muttered.

For dessert, she brought out a double chocolate cake that Diane thought looked very decadent. "Oh, Gladys, that looks yummy!"

"Good. You could use some fattening up."

"In that case, I'll have an extra-large piece." Diane suddenly remembered her skirt being a little lose on her this morning, which had surprised her.

"Are you not getting enough rest?" John abruptly asked.

"Of course I am, John. You know I am. You're both being silly, but I'll take a big piece of cake just to satisfy the two of you…not to mention me," she stated with a smirk.

"Good. I'll serve you first." Gladys cut a large piece for her, then glanced at John. "How about you? Are you hungry?"

"Like always, Gladys. I never turn down your desserts."

She cut him a portion, and as she served herself, John asked, "What do you hear from Dad lately?"

"Nothing much. Mildred told me he's not been feeling well recently."

John frowned. "What's going on? Any problems on his jobs?"

"No, Mildred didn't say that. I think Angi is wearing on him."

"That's nothing new. I think he realized really early in their marriage he'd made a mistake, but he didn't want to give up on it too fast."

"Divorce is a failure that is difficult to admit," Diane said quietly.

"Yeah, especially for Dad. I'll call him tonight after we get home."

The phone rang just then. It was his father, beating him to it.

Chapter Ten

"Is everything okay?" Diane asked when John came back to the table after talking to his father.

"Yeah. He had problems with the delivery of materials at a job site."

"Can you help him?"

"Yep, I told him who to call."

"So why do you still look worried?"

"Do I?" John asked. He shrugged. "I guess I was still thinking about Dad's health. But he'll be fine."

"Yes, of course." Somehow, as much as she wanted to believe him, she felt John wasn't telling her the truth. She hated even thinking that—that after everything they'd shared over the past six weeks, he'd keep things from her.

She suddenly stopped eating her chocolate cake.

"What's wrong, Diane?" Gladys quickly asked.

"Nothing, really. The cake is wonderful. I just lost my appetite."

"Are you feeling all right?" John asked, reaching out to touch her hand.

"Yes, I'm fine," she assured him, giving him a smile.

"I'd better get her home so she can get some rest," he said, standing. "Come on, honey."

"I want to help Gladys with the dishes."

"Nonsense, Diane. I have all night to finish the dishes," she declared. "Go home and put your feet up. Promise me that you'll get some rest."

Diane stood and hugged Gladys. "Don't worry about me. I'm fine."

She said nothing after she and John got in his car, just turned her head and stared out the window.

When they reached her apartment without speaking, she climbed the stairs slowly, feeling more and more exhausted.

"Diane, why don't you go get dressed for bed and then come watch television with me."

"I have some reading I need to do, John. It can't wait until tomorrow."

"Why didn't you tell me sooner? We could've stayed home tonight."

"Nonsense. I have plenty of time."

She put on a nightgown, something she hadn't done since he'd moved in with her, and crawled into bed with the papers she wanted to review.

All she could think about was the earlier conversation with Gladys.

She should've realized the woman would urge John to make their relationship permanent. But he had no intention of doing that. He liked being free to move in or out of relationships, and had no desire to make anything permanent. So tonight, in his own way, he had just let her know that soon they wouldn't be together anymore.

JOHN CAME INTO the bedroom after turning off the television. When he found Diane already asleep, he gathered her papers and put them in her briefcase by the front door. Then he crept back into the bedroom. He'd wanted to make love to her, but for some reason he didn't understand, she seemed in a funny mood tonight.

So he undressed and slid into bed beside her, pulling her into his arms. It wasn't the same as making love, but it would do. He just needed to be close to her.

Thinking back over the dinner conversation, he wondered if something was physically wrong with Diane. She had lost a little weight the last few days, but her appetite had slacked off a little.

The thought of her being ill was enough to cut him off at the knees. He couldn't bear that.

Maybe he should make her an appointment with Dr. Fielding. Everyone regarded him as the best doctor in Dallas. John had built a medical center for the man a few years ago. Surely he'd see Diane.

But then John would feel like a fool if she wasn't sick at all. No, he'd better just encourage her to see her own doctor. Then he'd discuss things with her.

The next morning, John tried to initiate lovemaking with Diane. She resisted, saying she was too tired. When he suggested she see her doctor, she dismissed his concern.

"I'm fine, John. Just because I don't have time to make love before going to work doesn't mean I'm sick."

"I didn't say that. But—"

"Maybe you need to find a girlfriend who doesn't work for a living! That would take care of your problem!" She bolted from the bed.

Following her, John caught her by the arm and pulled her to him.

"I don't want anyone but you, Diane. I just want you to take good care of yourself. If you need me not to be so demanding, then say so. I'll do whatever you want."

"No, John, I didn't mean that. I'm just a little tired this morning. Maybe if we stop going out during the week, except for dinner with Gladys, I won't get so crabby."

"Done. I'll call and cancel Elizabeth and Mark on Wednesday."

"No, don't cancel them. I like to meet them for dinner. It helps me relax."

"Okay, but we'll take a little downtime after that."

"Fine," she agreed, before kissing him goodbye.

He stayed at the door watching her go, thinking he should've stood up to her and canceled all their plans for a month or two. He had to be sure to take good care of her.

"Hey, John, how you doing?" a female voice cooed.

He looked over his shoulder to see Carolyn approaching, her sights set on him. "Fine. I'm off to work," he called, and jumped in his car and peeled out of the parking lot.

DIANE FELT UNSETTLED all day long. Surely she wasn't disturbed that much just because John hadn't wanted to make things permanent? No, she wasn't that bad. She'd known it was going to end sometime. And as she had told herself, she would have wonderful memories of the weeks with John.

But she hoped he'd tell her when he was leaving, and not drag it out. That would make it painful.

She concentrated on her work that day, looking for the satisfaction she'd always found in it. But concentration proved difficult.

"Diane, have a minute?"

She looked up to find Wendy at her door.

"Sure. What did you need?"

Wendy set some projections on her desk. "I think there's an error here somewhere. The numbers don't seem to jive."

Diane rechecked her work from yesterday and found her assistant was right. "Good catch. Thanks for calling that to my attention."

"I only noticed it because you've taught me so well, Diane." She smiled as she went back to her desk.

Diane pressed her lips together. How had she made such a stupid mistake? But she'd been tired yesterday, out of step. She had been for a while.

Maybe she should call her doctor, she thought, but then dismissed that as silly. Instead, she discussed it with Elizabeth when the two couples met for dinner two nights later.

"May I ask you a question, Elizabeth?" she said when the men excused themselves.

"Sure. Is something wrong?"

"I don't know. I wondered if after you and Mark started living together, did you get tired a lot? I seem to be exhausted."

Elizabeth laughed. "With three kids, I can't even remember when I wasn't tired. But, yeah, it's possible. After all, it takes a lot more effort to handle everything for two than it did for one."

"Of course, why didn't I think of that? I was afraid I was going out of my mind."

Elizabeth smiled. "I don't think you have anything to worry about. Unless you're pregnant, of course."

"No, that's not possible." She'd been on birth control for years, thanks to a terrible case of acne.

"I don't think John wants children, does he?"

"No, not at all."

"That's too bad."

"Yes, but at least he's honest about it."

"True, I hate men who lead you on."

They heard the men coming back in and switched to a safer topic.

When they got home, John took her to bed and just held her. "I talked to Mark about you being tired a lot. He said Elizabeth was the same way. It just took her awhile to get used to making love."

"I know. I asked Elizabeth, too."

"So we'll take it a little more slowly until you get used to it."

"And how do we know when that happens?"

"You'll be attacking me! Hey, that'll be fun. I could pretend to resist."

She slapped him on the arm. "Then I'd quit because I would think you didn't want me."

His expression went suddenly serious and his eyes darkened. "I'd never quit on you."

Those five words went straight to her heart, melting it on contact. She pulled him to her and made love to him as if she'd never let him go.

A FEW DAYS LATER, Diane had gotten home ahead of John for a change. She put her briefcase down and went to the kitchen to get a drink. Then she saw the answering machine blinking with three messages.

"John, it's Gladys. You need to call Mildred at once!"

"John, it's Gladys. I'm so sorry, but your dad collapsed this afternoon. They've taken him to the hospital. Meet Mildred there."

The last message confirmed Diane's fears. Doug had died at the hospital.

Just then, she heard John's key in the lock.

She wished more than anything he had come in first and she didn't have to tell him the news. But that was a cowardly thought.

Fighting back tears, she went to the door. Her voice trembled as she spoke. "John, your father collapsed at work today. They took him to the hospital, but—" And then she could stave them off no longer. The tears fell.

She saw his face as he absorbed her words. He went pale and grabbed her shoulders. "What are you saying?"

"He passed away, John. I'm so sorry!"

He pulled her against him and buried his face in her hair. His body felt stiff, rigid, as if in shock. When he stepped back, he muttered, "What do I do now?"

She wiped her tears. "I think Mildred is waiting for you at the hospital."

"Okay, I'll go. I'll let you know where I'll be tonight. I don't know if I'll get back here."

"I understand," Diane whispered. She kissed his lips and let him leave, wishing he'd ask her to come with him.

But he didn't.

JOHN WISHED he could've asked Diane to come with him. But he didn't want her to have to deal with Angi tonight, or even himself, overcome by disbelief, then grief. His father had had many faults, but John had loved him.

He'd hoped his dad would get through this rough spell and be happy. But that hadn't happened.

When John reached the hospital, he was directed upstairs, where he found Mildred sitting by herself in the hallway.

He whispered her name and she spun around, opening her arms to him as she always had when he'd been upset as a little boy.

"I'm so sorry, John. I brought him here as soon as he said he wasn't feeling well, but…they couldn't save him."

"I know, Mildred. Did he say anything?"

"He said you promised to deal with everything. And he said he thought Diane was the one for you."

"He never gave up, did he? He always thought I'd marry."

"No, Johnny," Mildred said, using the name she used to call him. "He only *hoped* you'd marry, like he did with your mother."

John swallowed and sat down.

"I told him not to worry about you, when you were little. That I would take care of you. But he thought you should have a mother."

"And you did take care of me, Mildred."

"It wasn't exactly a hardship, child."

He held her hand.

"Mr. Davis? Do you want to see your father now?"

John's head snapped up and he stared at the nurse in front of him. "Yes, thank you."

"I'll come with you, John," Mildred said, taking his arm as they went in.

They spent some time in the somber room, sharing memories of the man they'd both loved. When they left, John thought to ask about the new widow. "Where's Angi? Didn't she want to come to the hospital with you?"

"Get real, boy! She said to let her know how things went and, oh, could I fix her a sandwich before I left for the hospital?"

"Damn! I'm glad Dad is out of his misery, even if I do miss him. That woman needs to go."

"No, I'll be the one to go. She'll inherit the house and

half his fortune, probably. She certainly won't keep me around for any length of time."

"You're not going anywhere, Mildred. I'll make it clear that I pay your salary. She doesn't have the authority to fire you."

"Whatever you say, John. But there's no need to do me any favors. I can hardly stand the woman."

"That makes two of us." John took her hand and led her out of the hospital. "I'll follow you home and we'll face Angi together."

"If she's awake. I don't know if she really goes to sleep or if she just wanted to get away from your father, but she's goes up to bed early."

"I'll call her and have her stay up for us."

In the car, with his teeth clenched, John called his father's home. After a number of rings, Angi answered the phone.

"Hi, John. You haven't been over to see us lately. When are you coming by?"

"Right now, if it's not too late."

"Of course not. I'll get dressed and I'll be right down," she cooed.

"Right." John ground his teeth. She'd never even asked about her so-called beloved husband.

John couldn't wait to sink her ship.

Chapter Eleven

Diane didn't know what to do with herself. She paced around her apartment, wondering when John would call. When the phone rang, she raced to it, hoping it was him. Instead, it was his housekeeper.

"Oh, Gladys, have you heard from John?"

"No, I haven't, honey. He hasn't called you, either?"

"No."

"Have you eaten yet?"

"No, I—"

"Come have dinner with me. I've already got something fixed. There's no point in you staying there by yourself."

"You're sure you don't mind?"

"Honey, it would be a blessing to me."

"I'll be right there."

When Diane reached John's house, her first question dealt with John's whereabouts.

"I still haven't heard from him, Diane." Gladys put a motherly arm around her. "Come on, let's have some dinner. You look like you've lost weight."

"I'm fine, Gladys. I just haven't had much of an appetite lately. Been too busy, I guess."

"You've got to take care of yourself, honey," the woman told her, preceding her into the kitchen. "John seems so fond of you. He scarcely makes a move without you at his side."

Diane smiled, but shook her head. "He's still independent. It just happens that we both like the same things."

"I guess that's true. But it sure seems he'd rather have you beside him than anyone else."

Diane smiled again but said nothing.

"I thought Mildred would've called me by now, but it could be she's gotten mired down in paperwork. I've never handled a death before."

"Maybe she had to go back home to be with Angi? Or maybe Angi went with her to the hospital and had some problems."

"That woman wouldn't move her big toe to help anyone out," Gladys retorted sharply. "I'll bet she didn't even go to the hospital. And I'd bet more than John is glad his stepmother wasn't there!"

ON THE WAY to his father's house, John dialed Diane's number. He didn't really have much news, but he needed to hear her voice.

But there was no answer.

He couldn't think where she would be. It worried him that she didn't answer the phone. Should he swing by there to be sure she was all right?

No, he decided. That would show his weakness for her. He'd find her later...somewhere.

He followed Mildred's car into the driveway, then followed her into the house, expecting his father to greet him at any moment. When he realized that would never happen again, grief assailed him once more.

"You all right?" Mildred asked.

"Yeah. I—I just expected him to come meet me."

"I know. I'll see him in every room, I guess, for a while."

"Yeah. Where is the new widow?" he asked with heavy sarcasm.

Mildred moved to the intercom. "Angi, are you there?"

"Of course I am. Is John here?"

"Yes, he is."

"I'll be right down," she said, enthusiasm in her voice.

John looked at Mildred. "I'm going to have to talk to her alone, but stay close. She may get out of control and I'll need a witness."

"I'll put on a pot of coffee."

"Thanks, Mildred," he said, giving her a hug. Then he sat down at the head of the dining room table.

He heard running steps. Angi had never run to see his dad, as far as he knew. He squared his jaw.

"John, I'm so glad you're here," she said with a big smile. "How are you?"

"Not well, since my father just died."

Surprise flashed across her face, followed not by grief but nonchalance. "Oh. Well, I'm sure he's happy now."

John didn't bother to chastise her. All along he'd known she'd had no feelings for her husband. Now John just had to carry out his dad's requests.

"We need to talk," he said sternly. "Sit down."

She pulled out the chair next to him.

"Do you remember the prenuptial contract you signed before the marriage?"

Angi blinked several times. "Yes, of course, but since Doug died, it doesn't matter."

"You did read it, didn't you?"

"Yes, in front of that stuffy old lawyer Doug used. I had to sign a paper saying I did."

"According to that agreement, all you are to receive is half a million dollars. The house, of course, belongs to the estate. You can keep your car and any personal items. How long will it take you to move out?"

"No! That can't be true. I'm the widow. I get the house and maintenance. And—and half the estate."

John shook his head. "You only get what I've offered."

"You're wrong! You've got to be wrong! I'm carrying his child! Your own flesh and blood!"

"The child will be provided for."

Angi calmed down. "How much?"

"You will receive two thousand a month until the child is eighteen."

"Two thousand? That's absurd!"

"No, I'm afraid not."

Mildred came in with a coffee tray.

"Thank you, Mildred," John said. "You'll need to pack a bag. You'll be leaving with me tonight."

"Wait! Who's going to take care of me?" Angi demanded.

"How about you take care of you." John's demeanor remained calm. Angi, on the other hand, was becoming more and more agitated.

"But I can't be left here alone! I need Mildred to stay with me!"

"No. I know how you've abused her in the past. I'm not leaving her here with you. If you want to go to a hotel, I'll pay for a week there, and arrange a mover to pack your things. But I'll need a place to send them."

"Fine! I'll go to a hotel. I'm certainly not staying here. Mildred, go pack a bag for me."

But John shook his head. "Mildred is going to pack for herself. You'll have to manage on your own."

"Fine!" Angi exclaimed, and jumped to her feet. When she swayed momentarily, as if dizzily, John sat like a statue. He knew he couldn't give in the slightest bit. After shooting him a furious glare, Angi stomped out of the room.

John slumped in his chair and buried his face in his hands. He couldn't believe his father was dead. Now he had no one. Except Diane.

He pulled out his cell phone. When there was still no answer at her place, he sighed. Why didn't she have a cell phone? He'd have to change that. Then he remembered he'd better alert Gladys that Mildred was coming to stay there until things were settled.

When she answered the phone, John related the news to her.

"I'll fix up a room at once. Have you talked to Diane?" she asked.

"No! I can't find her."

"She just left here. I invited her over for dinner."

"Thanks, Gladys. I'll try her at home in a little while."

After he hung up his phone, he heard Mildred coming down the stairs.

She came into the room. "I'm ready, but I don't think we should leave until she does. She'll probably pack up all the silver."

"Good point. Would you mind going upstairs and helping her get her things together?"

"No, I don't mind."

"Thanks, Mildred."

He looked around at all the silver stored in open display cabinets. What was he going to do with everything? Maybe he could sell the house furnished. He could have the silver packed and sent to his house. And he'd want some personal mementos of his father. Maybe a painting or two.

Mildred and Angi came down the stairs together, Mildred carrying three suitcases, Angi with nothing. John stood at once and relieved Mildred of her burden. Then he handed the smallest bag to Angi.

"I can't carry it. I'm pregnant."

"I know. Carry it or leave it here. It doesn't matter to me."

As he expected, she grabbed it at once. He figured all the jewelry she'd conned out of his father must be in that bag. Carrying Mildred's case along with Angi's, he led the way out of the house.

As Mildred was locking the door, he asked Angi for her key. She reluctantly handed it over before storming off to her car.

When John arrived at his house, he accompanied Mildred inside. Then he asked her to call a locksmith and get the locks changed first thing in the morning.

"I'll take care of that, if you're sure, you want to," she agreed.

"I'm sure. I'm going to sell the house, and the proceeds will go into your retirement fund. Dad and I thought that would be some kind of reward for all you've put up with."

Mildred was left almost speechless. "That—that's too much, John!"

"No, it's not, Mildred. You took care of the house for years under difficult circumstances. Dad left you some money, too, but that can wait until the will is read."

John gave her a kiss on her cheek, thanked Gladys and hurried home to Diane.

When he got there, he looked at his watch. It was only ten-thirty, but there were no lights on in Diane's bedroom. Had she gone to bed early? He'd meant to call her again, but in the midst of trying to move Angi out and get Mildred situated, he had forgotten.

He went up the stairs and unlocked the door. The apartment was silent and dark. He made his way to the bedroom, undressed in the dark and slid into bed, up against Diane.

He eased his arm over her and pulled her just a little bit closer, giving thanks for the woman he'd found.

It was the first time he'd been warm since he'd gotten the news of his father's death.

Diane awoke before the alarm went off. She could feel John stirring next to her, and was glad for his warmth and the fact that he'd come home last night. Turning toward him, she cupped his cheek in her hand. "Are you okay?" she asked him, sympathetic for all he'd gone through. How she wished she could've been there for him last night.

"I'm okay now that I'm with you." He kissed her palm. "It was rough. I guess I never really thought what it'd be like to lose him. I was so young when my mother died, I barely even remember her. But my father…"

At the emotion in his voice, she reached out to comfort him. "I know, John. It must be hard. At least your dad didn't suffer."

"I know." He nodded slowly. "I just wish we would've had more time. That I hadn't let his wives keep me away."

"I'm sure he understood, John. Especially if they were all like Angi."

"Don't even remind me of her," he said, his eyes darkening. "She didn't even bother going to the hospital with Dad."

"I know. Gladys told me. I'm sure it made you angry."

"Very. I moved her out last night."

"Out of the house?"

"Yeah. I wouldn't leave Mildred there to wait on her. And I couldn't leave Angi there on her own. She would've packed up all the valuables before she left. So I put her bags in her car and sent her to a hotel."

"And she didn't complain?"

"No. She signed a prenup. Of course, she didn't really read it, but she swore in front of Dad's lawyer that she had and that she understood what it said. She thought that, as the widow, she would inherit everything."

"That must've been a rude surprise," Diane said, raising her brows.

"Yeah, almost as rude as the way she treated Dad." John looked away for a moment, then back at her. "But he liked you."

"I liked him, too."

The words seemed to ease his pain a bit and his brows unfurled. "I wish you'd known him longer."

"I'll know his son longer," she whispered, kissing him lightly. "You're a testament to the man he was."

He wrapped his arms around her, pulling her close. "I missed you last night."

"I missed you, too. But I'm glad you're here now." To show him how much, she kissed him again, till the alarm finally rang.

John silenced it. "I'll go fix breakfast while you shower."

"Thank you. I've gotten used to breakfast, since you make it every morning."

"I kind of like doing it," he said with a smile.

Diane slid out of bed and headed for the shower, even though she would've preferred to stay in bed with John. But he was in a funny mood this morning. She wasn't sure he wanted company. When she got to the bathroom and started the shower, she realized she wasn't feeling too well. Within seconds she lost the contents of her stomach.

Once the nausea passed, she sat on the toilet with the seat down. What had just happened? Did she have a touch of the flu? Or was it something she'd eaten at Gladys's last night?

It had to be flu. Diane hoped she didn't give it to John. Especially now, when he had so much to take care of.

After her shower, she dressed and went to the kitchen, where John had poured her a cup of coffee, and promptly presented her a plate piled high with bacon and blueberry muffins.

"Where did the muffins come from? You didn't make them this morning, did you?" she asked in surprise.

"Nope. Gladys made them after you left, and packed some up for me to bring home. She's afraid I'm not feeding you well. She mentioned that you didn't eat much last night."

"It was hard to get interested in food, thinking about your dad." Not that Diane felt much like eating now, though she picked at her muffin to appease him.

"Will you be late getting home today?" she asked.

"I'm not sure. Dad's got one project going on in

Denver. I may have to fly up there for a couple of days. Plus, I've got to check on his other developments. And keep mine going, and deal with Angi. I've also got the accounts for the other kids to check on. Dad put money away for each of them for college. I may give those to you to manage. Could you do that for me?"

"Of course, John."

"That'll be a big help. I'll get the papers and past history on those to you. There are the funeral arrangements as well."

"Can you meet me for lunch today?"

"I'll try, but it might have to be a quick one."

"That's fine," she assured him with a smile.

"You're wonderful, Diane. Very unflappable, and that helps me a lot right now."

After she'd kissed him goodbye, she drove to work, feeling a little lonely, though he hadn't even left for Denver yet. It was shocking how quickly she'd come to rely on his presence, his warmth, his caring.

With his father's death, though, their relationship was bound to go through a transition ahead. She hoped it would. But, as she'd always told herself, she knew it had to end some time. Just not now. She was enjoying life too much with John.

JOHN HEADED TO HIS DAD'S home. Mildred was supposed to be there, getting the locks changed. He wanted to be sure of that and to get the files on those accounts for his father's other children. He also needed to clear out his dad's safe. John didn't know if Angi knew the combination or not, but he wasn't taking any chances.

Doug Davis had been generous to his wives, but he'd always kept John's mother's jewels in the safe, never giving any away. John thought about Diane. Those things would look good on her.

His smile, brought on by thoughts of her, lasted until he reached his father's house. He found Angi on the doorstep, apparently waiting to enter.

"What do you want, Angi?" he asked.

"I forgot some things I want to get."

"Get me a list and I'll send them to you."

"But it would be so simple for me to just scoot in and get them," she said with a flirtatious smile.

"No." He walked around her, went in and closed the door before she could even protest. She beat on the door, but John didn't respond.

"What are we going to do about her?" Mildred asked, a frown on her face as she came to meet him.

"You're going to pack up anything of value, and I'm going to empty the safe this morning. Then there won't be anything here she wants."

"Okay. It'll only take another couple of hours to finish my part of the job. It's a good thing you got her figured out."

"Yeah. But I can't take a lot of credit. She's been pretty obvious for a long time."

"True. How's Diane this morning?"

"She's fine."

"Yes, she is. You need to be good to her."

"Mildred! I'm always good to my ladies…for a while."

"I think you need to make it permanent."

John was shocked at how good that advice sounded to him. "I'll keep that in mind," he said with a smile.

Then he went to his father's office and, after closing the door behind him, opened the safe. He loaded the papers and jewels into a duffel bag, zipped it, and then surveyed the room. His father had several paintings in here that John loved, partly because they brought back memories of his dad, and partly because they were western scenes of mountains and woods.

When he came out of the office, he carried two paintings he intended to take to his house, and the duffel bag. "Mildred? I'm going to the bank, then having a quick visit with Diane so I can hand over some papers. Then I'll go to Dad's office. If you need me, call me on my cell phone. I need you to call the Realtor I used on my last project, Rob Hopkins, and asked him to come look at the house and be prepared to meet with me tonight."

"I will, John. And you tell Diane hi from me."

"I will." He bent over and kissed her cheek. "You should go back to my house tonight. I don't want you staying here by yourself."

"Yes, John. You're a good boy."

He grinned. "Well, I do have my moments."

Chapter Twelve

Diane couldn't keep her mind on her work. Distracted as she was, she didn't notice Wendy until her assistant asked, "You feeling all right, Diane?"

She stopped short, the surprise no doubt showing on her face. "I—I'm fine," she lied, trying as ever to hide her personal life from her business associates.

But Wendy was too perceptive. "You look pale and…preoccupied. You're sure you're okay? Can I get you something?"

"Thanks anyway, but I'm fine." She looked to her office the way a drowning man eyes a lifeboat. "I've just got a lot of work to do today."

And get to work she did. With her door shut.

The morning passed in a blur of phone calls, meetings and computer work. She didn't even realize it was noon until she heard John's voice outside her door, telling Wendy that Diane expected him.

She got up and opened her door to them. "It's okay, Wendy. You can let Mr. Davis in."

Once her assistant left them, John stole a quick kiss that put Diane on edge. "I just need a minute before we head out to lunch," he told her.

"Come in, then," she said, waving him in and shutting the door behind him, eager for the privacy. "Can I do something for you?"

"For starters, you can store this duffel bag in your office. I used it to transport everything from my father's safe to a deposit box I opened downstairs." He handed it to her and watched her put it in a desk drawer. Then he reached inside his breast pocket for some official-looking documents. "Here are the files on the savings accounts my father set up for his other children. And a check to establish an account for Angi's baby."

"I'll take care of everything, John. Don't worry about these at all. I'll put them all in something safe but high yielding." She locked them in a file. "Now, are we ready to go to lunch?"

John came around the desk and pulled her into his arms. Before she could even consider her surroundings, he claimed her lips in a feverish kiss that she felt all the way to her toes.

"Now," he said, his voice husky, "I'm ready to go."

Diane put a hand on her desk to steady herself, needing a moment to gather her wits. John was already at the door when she remembered an earlier conversation she'd had with Mark.

"Mark Golan wanted to see you," she managed to say. "I promised I'd take you down when you got here.

He said he might want to come to lunch with us. He wishes to offer his condolences."

A frustrated expression flashed across John's face, but he followed her.

As soon as Mark saw him, he hugged John. "I'm so sorry to hear about your dad."

"Thanks, Mark. I appreciate your sympathy."

Mark, indeed, wanted to join them. When they were seated in a restaurant half a block away, eating lunch, he offered, "From what Diane told me, you've got a lot on your plate. Is there anything I can do to help?"

John sighed. "No, I can't think of anything. Dad's funeral is planned for Saturday morning at ten."

"I'll be there," Mark said.

John nodded and then looked at Diane. "You'll come, won't you, honey?"

"Of course I will, John."

"I want you to sit with me. I don't want Angi sobbing all over me. If I'm alone, she'll think I'm there to comfort her."

"If—if that's what you want." Diane tried to hide the hurt she felt at his words. He wanted her there for his protection? Not because he was sharing his grief with her.

Mark picked up on it, too, apparently. "That's a little cold, John."

"You don't know Angi," John retorted.

"But—"

"It's all right, Mark." Diane stopped his argument with a small shake of her head.

"What? What are you talking about, honey?" John asked.

"Nothing. You've got a lot on your mind."

He rubbed his face with both hands. "Yeah," he agreed. "Look, I won't see you until the funeral, but I'll pick you up at nine-thirty Saturday morning."

"All right," she said, remaining calm.

"Then I'd better go. Thanks for meeting me," he said to Mark. He bent and kissed Diane briefly, and walked out of the restaurant, leaving the two bankers behind.

"Are you all right?" her colleague asked. "I can't believe he didn't realize how cold he sounded."

"It doesn't matter, Mark. He needs me there, for whatever reason, and I've seen Angi in action. She's hoping to snare John."

"Well, that won't happen."

"You never know, Mark. She is carrying his father's child."

"I don't think John will end up married to her. Hell, he doesn't intend to marry anyone."

"I know," Diane said, as she stood and picked up the bill.

"Here, Di, I'll pay for it. I can write it off."

"So can I. Come on, I need to get back to work."

After she paid, she and Mark walked back to the bank. As soon as they entered the building, she excused herself and headed to the closest bathroom, barely making it before she lost her lunch in the first sink. She washed her face and cleaned the basin.

Then she realized she felt fine. No more sickness. That was odd. She would have to be careful what she ate for a day or two.

She went back upstairs to her office. Today was Thursday. She wanted to take care of this new work of John's before the weekend. Besides, working would be better than sitting around wondering if he would be in her life next week.

JOHN MET WITH THE REALTOR that night at his father's house, about eight o'clock.

"Look, Rob, I'd like to sell it furnished, but if you can't, I'll get it cleaned out," he said.

"Well, this is a great house, John. I'm sure I can sell it, but it may take a little time. And it is very nicely furnished."

"Thanks, Rob. I appreciate your handling the sale."

"I'm delighted you called me. I'll start advertising it right away."

John shook his hand and showed him out. Then he turned and went back up the stairs. Angi had left a list with Mildred of things she wanted from the house. Most of it John ignored. The paintings that had hung in her room had not been bought specifically for her. They had hung there for years before her entrance to the Davis home.

However, she listed several personal items, including some makeup and jewelry, that were hers. He found the items and put them all in a bag.

Then he left the house for the last time.

He thought about going to Diane's, but something made him hesitate.

He wanted her so badly, and the need scared him. When it came to Diane he was not in control, and that wasn't a feeling John tolerated.

Instead, he headed back to his own house. He gave Mildred the things Angi wanted, at least what he was willing to let her have, and he went to bed. Tomorrow he had to look after his father's company, to visit each job site to let the men know their employment, at least until that particular job was completed, was safe.

Decisions would have to be made in the long term, but he was dealing with the immediate future as best he could. The thought that a night with Diane would make him stronger was shoved out of his mind.

DIANE WAS SICK the next morning before she even dressed or ate anything. She skipped breakfast and went to work on an empty stomach. When it happened again on Saturday morning, she decided to see her doctor on Monday. In the meantime, she had to get ready for Doug Davis's funeral.

She chose a black suit. It disturbed her that the waist of the skirt was a little loose on her. It had been a perfect fit the last time she'd worn it. She chose a gold lapel pin to relieve the blackness.

At nine-thirty, she heard a knock on the door. She opened it and found John standing there, dressed in a somber black suit.

"Why did you knock? Did you lose my key?"

"No, but I felt a little strange just walking in on you. I thought it would be better to knock."

A sense of dread tightened her stomach at his words, and at the fact that he greeted her without a kiss. But she said nothing, just "Did you eat a good breakfast?" he asked as he followed her down the stairs.

"Yes, I did," she lied.

"I don't think I believe you, but Gladys and Mildred are preparing some food for afterward. You can eat something then."

Diane said nothing. Until she found out what was upsetting her stomach, she'd have to be careful what she ate.

When they reached the church where services for Doug Davis would be held, John led her around to a side door, to the room where the family would gather. They would be led in to the service after everyone was seated.

Mildred and Gladys were there, as well as Angi and the other ex-wives, plus three little dark-haired boys.

John spoke to each of his father's wives and his half brothers, introducing Diane to them. When he reached Angi, he said, "Of course, you already know Angi, Diane."

"What's she doing here? She's not family!" Angi protested.

"I invited her."

"But I expected—hoped you'd escort me. This is such a difficult moment for me."

"It might've been less difficult if you'd gone to the hospital with my father the night he died."

The other three wives stared at Angi. One of them said, "You didn't even go with him?"

"I didn't feel well," Angi explained, not very convincingly.

John turned away. He wanted no more conversation with Angi. Holding Diane's hand, he led her over to Mildred and Gladys. Mildred had tears in her eyes, and Diane put a comforting arm around her.

Doug's housekeeper smiled. "He was a good man."

"I know," Diane said. "And I'm sure he appreciated your dedication."

Then she sat down beside Gladys. "This is an interesting family group, isn't it?" she asked softly.

"Yeah," John's housekeeper whispered back. "They all look the same, don't they?"

Diane looked at the four women across from her. Gladys was right. They represented the quintessential society woman in five-year increments, their makeup the same, their surgically repaired beauty obvious. How sad that Doug hadn't found a woman who loved him for himself rather than because of his net worth.

No wonder John had such a terrible attitude toward marriage. He'd seen his father betrayed by all these women. Though Diane recognized that part of the problem had been Doug's, she wasn't sure John could or ever would realize it.

Her gaze moved to the three little boys. The oldest looked to be about fifteen, the middle one eleven or twelve and the youngest eight or nine. None of them had played a big part in Doug Davis's life, she would guess.

Though John was kind to them, he didn't spend much time with the boys. However, he gathered them around him to talk for a couple of minutes before the minister came in.

John stood and greeted the pastor. He introduced Doug's family to him, starting with the three boys, who gravely shook the man's hand, even though the youngest one probably had no idea who the man was.

Then John introduced his father's four wives. The minister expressed his sympathies, but they moved through that group quickly. John then brought the reverend to Mildred and Gladys, and lastly, Diane.

"Miss Black, I'm delighted to meet you. John told me how helpful you've been."

"Thank you." Diane couldn't imagine what John had said, but she certainly wasn't going to ask. She smiled and sat back down beside Gladys.

Diane watched as John talked quietly to the minister for several minutes. She hoped he would come back to her side and hold her hand. She'd feel so much better then.

A few minutes later, the minister returned to lead them into the main chapel. Diane was seated beside John in the front row, with Gladys and Mildred. Angi had tried to join them, but the minister had insisted she sit in the second row with Doug's ex-wives. She tried to whisper to John, but he ignored her.

The service began and John reached out and took Diane's hand, holding it against his thigh. She reveled in his warmth throughout the service.

Afterward, John whisked her out to his car and they drove the short distance to his house. Gladys and Mildred were right behind them. Diane joined the two women in the kitchen and helped them keep the serving plates full and drinks available for the guests.

Diane took a special interest in the three boys, who each looked a little like John. They were charming and she enjoyed visiting with them. Tom, the middle child, who was eleven was the most outspoken. "Were you married to our dad, too?" he asked, his mouth full of food.

"No, sweetie, I'm just a friend of John's."

Tom nodded, but the oldest boy, Matt, struck up his courage to admit, "John scares me a little."

She came to his defense. "I don't think he intends to scare you. He's just not used to being around children."

Zachary, the nine-year-old, swallowed his milk and said, "Well, I like him."

"I like him, too," Diane agreed.

"So do I," said Gladys, as she stopped by the table with a tray in each hand. She smiled at Diane. "Did you eat?"

"I will, Gladys," she promised. Her stomach seemed settled now, but she'd be careful about what she tried to eat. She left the boys and returned to the kitchen. "Mildred, you should sit down and let Gladys and me handle things for a while."

"No, child, I'm better off working. I don't want to think about Doug. Here, have some food. Gladys says you've been losing weight. We can't have that. Soon you'll just blow away."

Diane laughed. "I doubt that. But I'll take one of those roast beef sandwiches you made." She smiled.

"I'm glad I'm not trying to lose weight, Mildred. You'd really make it hard."

John came into the kitchen just then. His face looked tight and his eyes dark. He appeared exhausted, as if running on empty. Everyone here today wanted a piece of him, wanted to express their condolences and offer help. But John wasn't one to take it. he almost looked past her as he came in for some more glasses. "How are you doing?" he asked distractedly, never really seeing her.

"I'm fine, John. Don't worry about me."

He grabbed a tray of clean glassware and headed back out, stopping only long enough to say, "I probably won't be able to take you home for at least a few hours." Then he was gone.

Diane sat there speechless, the sandwich halfway to her gaping mouth. Since the service, John hadn't spoken to her for two minutes. And she'd just been blown off.

Gladys broke the awkward silence. "I can take you home once things slow down around here."

"Nonsense. You'll be exhausted. I'll just call a cab." She got up to do so, figuring now was as good a time as any to leave. It wasn't as if John cared if she stayed. But Elizabeth came into the kitchen then, saying her husband would be glad to drive her.

"It would be something Mark can do for John. He wants to help out so badly. Please?"

Diane accepted the offer.

Ten minutes later Mark came to get her. "John's in the library with some of his father's friends. You want to say goodbye?"

Did she? Would John care? If she didn't say goodbye, would he even notice she was gone?

Probably not.

"No, it's all right, Mark," she decided. "Let's just go."

With that, she left the house, thinking that it might be her last time there.

Chapter Thirteen

"Don't you even care that Diane left?"

Gladys waylaid John on his umpteenth trip into the kitchen an hour later. He looked up at her harsh words, his eyes scanning the room. "Where'd she go?" he asked, just realizing she was absent.

Clearly, his housekeeper was not pleased with him. "Mark took her home. He did your job." Gladys lifted her chin in the air.

"If Mark took her home, I'm sure she'll be all right," John said defensively.

"I hope so. She didn't look too happy."

"It's a funeral, Gladys, not a party!" John snapped.

His housekeeper glared at him and might have said more, but a guest entered the kitchen to get a refill on his drink.

John took the opportunity to slip away. In truth, he felt a little guilty about how he'd treated Diane. It hadn't been intentional, he assured himself. Then he admitted that maybe it had.

The power she had over him was making him nervous. He wanted to prove to himself that he could take her or leave her, but so far, all he'd proved was that he needed her. She calmed him and made him feel good.

That wasn't love…was it?

He had so little to go by. Once, in college, he'd thought he was in love. And he'd thought the young woman felt the same. But when his father had told her that his son wouldn't inherit anything from him, she'd begun to hedge her bets. Eventually, she'd found a wealthier young man and told John she'd changed her mind, she didn't love him, though she'd told him many times before that she did.

His father had talked to him about the dangers of marrying a woman looking for an easy life. Doug Davis should know; he'd managed to marry four such women after John's mother died. Each of them had seen him as a meal ticket.

Diane wasn't like that. She had a career, earned good money, didn't ask for promises. He'd had to persuade her to come to his house. She preferred that he come to hers, and he'd agreed. Damn it, he'd agreed!

Okay, so after he got everything settled, maybe they should change the rules a little. She couldn't have everything her way. He had needs, too.

But she'd met his needs, he suddenly realized. She'd been there for him. She'd supported him at the funeral, even when he'd told her why he needed her with him. That thought almost brought him to his knees.

When he dealt with women, he always couched things in proper terms, not being honest with them. He manipulated them. But he hadn't done that with Diane. She hadn't complained about it. Had she been upset?

Why *didn't* she complain, make demands?

He thought about what he knew of her past. She'd been ignored by her parents, had no other family. She'd learned to depend on no one but herself.

Feeling like scum, he immediately reached for the phone. But then he turned away. He wasn't ready to talk to her yet. If he did, he'd probably be honest with her again, and that didn't seem like a safe choice.

He'd call her later.

DIANE DIDN'T HEAR FROM John until Sunday afternoon, just before he left for Denver.

"Diane, it's John. How are you?"

"Fine," she said, maintaining a stiff upper lip, because she was feeling below par.

"Look, I'm sorry about the way I asked you to sit beside me at the funeral. I realized I sounded very selfish—"

"It's all right, John. I understood."

"Yeah, well, I—I'm heading out to Denver in a little while. I'm sorry I didn't get by to see you. There's just been so much to get done."

"Yes, of course. How long will you be gone?"

"A couple of days. I'll let you know before I show up on your doorstep."

"You're always welcome, John. I—I've missed you."

"I've missed you, too, honey. Things will settle down soon. Just hang on."

She could only hope.

MONDAY MORNING, as soon as she reached the office, Diane called her doctor's office. They promised to squeeze her in as soon as she could get there. She grabbed her purse and hurried to Wendy's desk to let her know where she'd be.

"You're sick?"

"I think it's a touch of the flu, but I just want to be sure."

"Oh, of course. I'll cover for you."

"Thanks, Wendy."

In ten minutes she was at the doctor's office, telling the nurse the symptoms she'd been experiencing.

The nurse put her through all the preexamination routines, including blood pressure test and a urinalysis. When she put Diane on the scale, there was no denying the weight loss; she'd dropped five pounds. She almost laughed to herself, thinking of how many times she'd tried to lose that weight and hadn't. Now she didn't even know how she'd done it. Was she badly sick?

The nurse escorted her into an examination room, decorated cheerily in yellows and blues. But the decor did little for Diane; the longer she waited, the more nervous she got. By the time her doctor entered, she was a wreck.

"I understand you've been experiencing some nausea and lost weight," he said once the amenities were over. He flipped through the papers in her chart. "Well, I think I've discovered the problem."

He paused and Diane twisted her hands tightly together.

"I hope it's good news," he said. "You're pregnant."

She leaped to her feet. "What? But I can't be!"

"Are you saying you haven't had unprotected sex recently?"

Diane sank back onto the table. "I—I take birth control pills…. For my complexion. I have for years."

"What strength are they?" he asked as he looked through her records. "Oh, yes, I see it here. That strength isn't as high as it should be to keep you from getting pregnant."

"B-but the last time, I didn't—I mean, this isn't the first time I've had sex, and I didn't get pregnant before!"

The doctor shrugged. "Diane, even birth control pills aren't a hundred percent effective. But the next time, I'd take a higher level of protection. Now, what do you want to do about the baby? My guess is you're about a month along. Do you want to keep it?"

Diane stared at him. What was he asking her? Her brain was scrambled. Suddenly she realized he wanted to know if she wanted an abortion. "No!" she exclaimed, her hand going to her stomach.

"No, you don't want to keep it?"

"Yes, I want to keep it." She drew a deep breath as she waited for his response.

"Good. I'm glad to hear it."

"But I will have to move away," Diane said, thinking aloud.

But where would she go? Dallas was the only home she'd ever known.

"Why would you have to do that?"

"I'm not married."

"I realize that, but maybe the father—"

"No! I'm not going to tell him."

"But then he'd pay child support."

"No! No, that's not necessary."

"But, Diane, it's the law. He won't be the first man caught in that situation. It will be all right."

Diane would hear none of it. She put up a hand to halt the line of conversation. "I'll let you know where to send my files."

"You're serious about leaving?"

"Yes, I have no choice."

"But I don't understand."

Diane smiled at him. "I know."

"Well, at least let me get you started on some pills that will help you keep your food down, hopefully."

That would help, she thought.

"And I'm also giving you a prescription for vitamins. Be sure and take one every day."

"I will. Doctor, there's no mistake, is there? I really am pregnant?"

"You really are pregnant. If you don't move away, I'll expect to see you in one month. Make the appointment with my nurse. You can always cancel if you need to."

"All right. Thank you, Doctor."

"Don't give up on the nausea pills. They need to build up strength to reach their full potential."

"How long do I need to take them?"

"You can stop every once in a while to see if you still get sick, but if you do, go back on them. You won't need them for more than three months, I don't think."

"Thank you," Diane said, her mind plowing through what she was going to have to do—at once.

The doctor handed her a stack of pamphlets. "These may answer any questions you have. But if you're worried about anything, just give me a call."

She shook his hand. "Thanks."

As she walked to her car, Diane was frantically making lists in her mind. Once she sat down behind the wheel, she took a pad and pen and made some notes. She didn't have time to make mistakes. Everything had to be done so quickly.

Once she reached Guaranty National, she went to the bank president's office and told his secretary she had an emergency and needed to see Mr. Harvey at once.

After a quick consultation with her boss, the secretary let Diane into his office. For only a few minutes, she warned.

Diane ignored her. Whether she stayed long or not, she had something to accomplish.

Mr. Harvey stood and smiled, gesturing to one of the chairs in front of his desk. "My secretary said you had an emergency, Diane. How can I help?"

"I would like to transfer to our bank in Atlanta." She'd decided on Atlanta because it was the only place she'd been to that she could see herself living.

The executive frowned. He liked Diane, but more importantly, she was good for the bank. That wasn't what he wanted to hear.

"Well, now, Diane, why would you want to do that? Do you need a raise? I think I can—"

"Mr. Harvey, I'm going to Atlanta. I'd like to have a job there, but if not, I'll manage. I'm leaving tomorrow."

"Can't I talk you out of it?"

"No, you can't." She sat tall in her chair. "Can you help me with a job there?"

"I'll have to make some phone calls," he said in a clipped voice. "Aren't you even going to give me a reason for this change?"

She stood. "I'm sorry, I can't. Please call me when you have an answer." With a quick handshake she left his office.

When she got to her own office, she called Wendy to help her. "Wendy, please don't tell anyone, but I'm leaving, and I need you to help me pack up my personal items. While you're doing that, I'm going to make a list of what will need to be handled right away here, and a list of investments I've recently made."

"You're leaving? But why?"

"I can't tell you, so please don't ask, and don't tell anyone else."

"When are you going?" Wendy inquired, almost on the verge of tears.

"Today."

Her colleague gasped, but Diane ignored her. She was on a mission to provide for her child. Nothing else mattered.

The two women worked side by side for almost an hour. Diane had just decided she'd left things in the best order she could manage when the phone rang.

It was Mr. Harvey. "Diane, I've made the arrangements for you in Atlanta. You'll report to the president of the bank, Mr. Wilborough. What day will you be there?"

"Next Monday. And I really appreciate your helping me, Mr. Harvey."

"I just wish I knew why."

And she wished she could tell him. But she couldn't.

After she hung up the phone, she looked at Wendy. "I'm going to leave now. Thanks for helping me."

Her assistant hugged her, with tears rolling down her cheeks.

"Don't cry, Wendy. I'm sure your next boss will really appreciate your assistance. I know I did."

"Th-thank you," Wendy stuttered.

Diane picked up the box with her belongings and headed out the door. In the elevator, she set it on the floor. It was really too heavy to carry very far. When the elevator door opened on the ground floor, she hoisted the box and exited, hoping to get out of the bank building before encountering anyone she knew.

As luck would have it, Mark Golan was right there in the lobby. "Diane, here, let me help you with that box," he exclaimed.

"Thank you, Mark, but I can manage."

"Nonsense. Where are you taking it?"

"To my car. But I can carry it."

"No, I will. Elizabeth would never forgive me if I didn't help you."

Diane said nothing else. She held open the door for him and he followed her out and down the sidewalk toward her car.

"I really appreciate the help, Mark," she said as they reached it.

"Diane, it's none of my business, but it looks like you've cleaned out your desk. And the only reason for that is—"

"I'm leaving, Mark. I hope you won't spread that around. I'm transferring to another branch."

"You are? But what about John? I mean, I thought—"

"No. We all knew it was temporary. John always moves on."

"You've talked to him?"

"Of course."

"Okay," Mark said slowly. "Well, Elizabeth and I will miss you."

Diane was suddenly engulfed with emotion. "I'll certainly miss you and Elizabeth. Tell her...I'll call her in a few days."

"All right. Good luck, Diane," Mark said, giving her a brief hug. He stood there watching as she drove off.

When she reached home, she found the name of the moving company she wanted to use and called them. It took some effort to convince them to accept the short notice, but finally they agreed to come out in the morning prepared to pack.

Then she lay down on her bed—for just a few minutes, she told herself. Her energy was flagging.

It was two hours later when she awoke. Appalled that she'd wasted so much time, she made herself a late lunch and then remembered the pills she needed to pick up. She grabbed the prescriptions and hurried to the drugstore. Then she drove to the nearest gas station and filled up her car, so she wouldn't have to stop tomorrow when she was all loaded down.

Back at home, she cleaned out her pantry and refrigerator and knocked on the flight attendants' door across the hall, offering them everything except the one frozen dinner she planned to eat for supper. Surprised, the six women took the extra food and expressed sorrow that she was leaving.

Diane dredged up a smile, but said little, sidestepping all their questions.

When she went back to her apartment, though, the smile faded. She was going to miss this place on Yellow Rose Lane. The fourplex had been her home since college, and for the most part she'd been happy here.

But now it was time to go.

She began packing her clothes, systemically going through her closet. After filling three suitcases, she took a quick shower, trying not to think about the shower she'd shared with John.

She pressed her palms to her stomach, though there was no sign of the baby yet. But all she'd done today was for her child. She was running away for the sake of this unborn infant. She'd known she'd have to live without John in her life. He'd been pulling away all week.

It had come too soon, in Diane's opinion. Yet, ironically, at the perfect time. She could disappear without having to reveal her secret. He need never know he'd fathered a child.

She wouldn't feel guilty about concealing his baby

from him. He had told her over and over that he never wanted children or even to get married.

She was only doing what he wanted.

As if her thoughts conjured him, he called her on the phone.

"Hi, John," she said, struggling to keep any emotion from her voice. "Are you still in Denver?"

"Yeah, I'll be home tomorrow night."

"Oh, good."

"Is everything all right?"

"As far as I know. I haven't actually talked to Gladys or Mildred, but I'm sure they're fine."

"I just spoke to them," he told her.

Ah. She was second. No matter, she told herself.

Silence fell between them. Diane didn't know what to say. She couldn't speak of the baby growing inside her, or her plans to protect that child. She couldn't ask him to come see her when he got back to town. She wouldn't be here.

"Well, I just thought I'd check on you. Gladys was afraid you'd forget to eat."

"No, I won't forget to eat."

"Then I'll see you when I get back."

"Have a safe trip."

She hadn't even had to lie to him. Such a mild, bland conversation with the man she loved.

She sank down on the sofa. What had she just admitted? She couldn't love him! But she did. And always would, as the father of her child. Tears rolled down her cheeks. She'd known their breakup would hurt. But she had been concentrating so deeply on the baby that the pain hadn't hit her until now.

It hurt much more than she'd thought.

She wrapped herself in a blanket from her bed and curled up in a ball on the sofa, tears streaming down her face. For the first time ever, she'd given herself completely to a man she'd fallen in love with. And now he was out of her life.

Rocking back and forth, she mentally reviewed their relationship, lingering over the feelings she'd discovered within herself because John had touched her, physically and emotionally.

But gradually she calmed down. She had to be strong now, for her baby. It was her job to protect and love this child more than anything. She wanted to do what her parents hadn't done.

Would she have a boy? she suddenly wondered. Angi had said the Davis men had sons. Diane thought she'd fare better with a girl, because she knew more about them. But if her child was a boy, she'd still love him. Totally and completely.

She slowly got up from the sofa and put the frozen dinner in the microwave. She'd have to learn to cook better balanced meals again. She used to cook more, but somehow, as her responsibilities at work grew, she'd spent less time in the kitchen.

After eating her dinner, she took the pill that might allow her to keep down her food, and then she went to bed.

Diane was so tired, she never heard the phone ring half an hour later.

Chapter Fourteen

John paced the floor in his hotel room, trying to understand what was going on inside him. Diane was fine. He'd just talked to her. So why was he fighting the urge to call her again?

Because they hadn't said anything that mattered. She hadn't demanded anything of him. Neither had he asked anything of her. He felt a need to hear her say she cared for him. Surely she could at least tell him that. He picked up the phone and dialed her number.

It rang about six times but she never answered. John hung up the phone and paced again in frustration. Maybe she'd run to the store for something. He'd try again later.

He'd just walked away from the phone when it rang. He raced to grab it, certain it was she.

"Diane?"

"Sorry to disappoint you. It's Mark."

"Hi, Mark. How are you?"

"Confused and a little angry."

"What about?"

"About Diane leaving. I know you don't stay too long with any one woman, but Diane is special, and I don't think you did the right thing, dumping her like this."

John froze. Finally, he said, "What are you talking about?"

"I'm talking about Diane leaving the bank. I helped her carry out a box a little before noon. It obviously had her belongings from her desk."

"What? Did she get fired? Who can I call? I'll take care of it. Just tell me who to phone."

"The one you need to call is Diane. I talked to Wendy, her assistant. Well, I wasn't exactly honest with her. I told her Diane had told me about her leaving. She filled me in on what happened. I know Diane had a doctor's appointment this morning. But when she got back, she went to the president's office and asked him to transfer her to Atlanta. By the way, I'm not supposed to tell you that. Anyway, he tried to get her to stay, even offered her a raise. She said she was leaving for Atlanta tomorrow, with or without a job. He scrambled to keep her in the company, and found her a position there. She starts next Monday."

John felt as if his brain had been scrambled. "This doesn't make sense. I talked to her tonight. Everything was fine."

"Did you ask her if she was staying put?" Mark asked.

"No, but she didn't say she was leaving. Surely she'd tell me if she was."

"Do you have some kind of an agreement?"

"Of course not! I'd never give a woman the power to hold me."

"So you have no hold over her? You're okay with her going?"

"No!" John retorted. "She's supposed to be there. Or at least let me know if she's leaving!"

"What's good for one is good for the other," his friend said softly. "Surely you learned that from your father. One-sided affairs never work."

"Damn it, it wasn't one-sided! We both—" John broke off, unsure what to say. Unsure what he felt.

"I've got to think," he muttered, said as much to himself as to Mark. "Has Elizabeth talked to her?"

"No. I thought about having her call, but I didn't know what to do, either. You could've been happy that she wasn't hanging on."

"No, I'm not happy. I thought… What does her trip to the doctor have to do with what happened today?" he suddenly asked.

"I don't know. She didn't look ill. Well, a little pale, but not sick."

"She's been losing weight. Gladys has mentioned it several times."

"I don't know anything about women's illnesses."

"Let me talk to Elizabeth for a minute."

"Okay, I'll get her."

John sat there, frustration building. He *would* have to be out of town when something like this happened. He wanted to grab Diane and shake her until she confessed what she was doing.

"Hello?"

"Elizabeth, this is John. Mark and I were talking, but we really don't know about female things. Diane went to the doctor, came back to the bank and quit her job, apparently. What could the doctor have said that would make her leave?"

"Has she been sick lately?"

"She's lost some weight, kind of been off her feed, you know?"

"How long has she been losing weight?"

"Just the last week or two."

"Hmm, has she been nauseous?"

"I don't think so. Not that I've noticed. I haven't been… I mean, you know, I was mostly busy with my dad's things."

"Yes, of course. I saw her the day of the funeral and she seemed a little subdued. Did you two have a falling out?"

"No. I mean, I may have been a little thoughtless, but I would've made it up to her."

"Well, the only thing I can think of that fits what you've told me is when I got pregnant."

John's heart stood still. Then he asked, "You *lose* weight when you get pregnant?"

"Some women do. I did, but then I was throwing up every morning for a while. If Diane hasn't been sick, I'm not sure what could be wrong."

"Well, she couldn't be pregnant. She's on birth control pills. So it must be something else."

"I couldn't tell you, then, John."

"Would you do me a favor?"

"I'll try. What do you want?"

"I want you to go over in the morning and talk to her. See what you can find out, and delay her as long as you can. I'll be taking the first flight out and I'll get there as soon as I can. I don't want to lose her."

"Okay. I'll go. I wanted to see her before she leaves, anyway."

"Thanks, Elizabeth," John said.

After he hung up the phone, he called the airline to change his reservation. The earliest flight out was seven o'clock the next morning. It would take a little over two hours to reach Dallas.

Could he remain calm for the two-hour flight? Maybe they'd let him pace up and down the aisles. He didn't know how else he'd manage to pass the time.

What if she left before he could get there?

No, he wasn't going to think about that. He'd arrive in time and he'd talk her out of leaving. John thought about calling Gladys and Mildred and sending them over to Diane's, too. But that might be too much. When they reconciled, he'd want to take her upstairs and make love to her. Gladys in particular wouldn't want them to do that. She'd think he should marry Diane first.

First? Had he changed his mind about marriage? He would admit that he could consider marriage if that was the only way she'd stay.

But she'd never asked him to marry her. Why would that be important now?

He kept coming back to her visit to the doctor. Something had happened there that he didn't know about. But he'd find out.

He would.

DIANE DIDN'T TRY eating breakfast the next morning. The moving company was coming at nine, so she set her alarm for eight. When it went off, she had to fight with herself to get out of bed. Why was she so tired? She'd gone to sleep early last night.

Maybe it had something to do with the pregnancy. She picked up the brochures the doctor had given her, and almost at once found an article explaining a new mother would experience exhaustion for at least the first three months.

"Aha! I guess that's the reason."

Though she wasn't leaving until around noon, she had planned on driving at least eight hours today. She wasn't sure she could do so that long. If she had to take an extra day to make the trip, she would.

A glance at her watch had her scrambling to get dressed. She had just combed her hair when there was a knock on her door. She hurried to open it.

"Miss Black?" the man asked.

"Yes?"

"I'm Gene Cowers from the moving company. Can I come in?"

"Of course." She led the way into her living room. "Do you want the tour first?"

"Uh, yes, ma'am. You want us to pack everything?"

"Please. I've packed my clothes, but I didn't know

until yesterday that I was moving. I start my new job next Monday, so I need to get there as soon as possible and find a place to live."

"They didn't give you much time," the man said with a frown.

Diane just smiled.

After they walked through the apartment, they sat down at the breakfast table and went over the details, which took longer than Diane had thought. When they finished, it was already ten-thirty.

"Shall we start packing now?"

"Yes, please. Oh, and could I get someone to carry down my three bags?"

He gave her a strange look, but agreed at once to do so.

Just as they reached the ground level, a car pulled into the parking lot and Elizabeth Golan got out.

"Elizabeth! What—"

"I wanted to say goodbye, Diane, and make you promise to send me your new address once you get settled." She paused and looked at the man. "I'm sorry if I'm interrupting something."

"No, this gentleman is from the moving company. He and his crew are going to pack up my things. I asked him to carry down my bags for me."

"How nice of you," Elizabeth said to him. Then she turned to Diane. "Have you eaten breakfast?"

"No, I haven't, but—"

"Then come have breakfast with me. There's a little pancake house just a couple of blocks away. It won't take long."

Diane couldn't resist Elizabeth's request. She was really going to miss her. "Okay, just for a few minutes."

Elizabeth turned to the man. "If anyone comes for her, just tell them she'll be back in a few minutes."

Diane gave her a strange look. "No one's going to come, Elizabeth. You and Mark and my assistant are the only ones who know. I don't think Mr. Harvey went around telling people."

Her friend laughed. "Probably not. I just felt a little guilty taking you away. But I'm so glad you've agreed. Come on, I'll drive."

Diane got in Elizabeth's car, wondering if she should've refused the invitation. But Elizabeth had become such a good friend. And taking half an hour out of her day couldn't hurt anything.

When they were seated in a corner booth in the pancake house, Elizabeth said, "I'm going to forget my diet this morning and order pancakes. How about you?"

Diane looked at the menu. Maybe plain pancakes would be okay. "I'll join you."

"Good. Then Gladys can't complain about you losing weight. I think it's wonderful the way you get along with her and Mildred."

"They're both very sweet women. I think if Doug had married Mildred after John's mother died, he might have been happy."

"Did she love him? I wondered about that."

"She never said so, at least not in that context. But she certainly cared about him. I think she's a wonderful lady. She's living at John's right now while they sell the house."

"Is she going to stay there for a long time?"

"I don't know. John said something about giving her the value of Doug's house for her retirement fund."

"That would be a nice fund!"

"I think she earned it. I wouldn't have wanted to work for Angi or any of the others."

"No, but she got to take care of the children, I guess."

"Yes," Diane agreed with a small smile. She could still picture the three little boys' faces, much like their older half brother.

When the waitress came to take their orders, Diane asked for a cup of hot tea. Elizabeth teased her about not having coffee, but Diane told her she was already awake, and didn't need coffee. The drinks arrived almost at once. Diane opened her purse and took out her vitamin.

"What's that?" Elizabeth asked.

"Vitamins. I went to my doctor and he suggested I take these," she said, carefully shielding the label from Elizabeth's gaze.

"Oh, that's good. Especially with the move."

The waitress returned with their pancakes.

Unlike Elizabeth, Diane added no syrup to her stack of pancakes. She cut off a small bite and ate it slowly.

"What kind of place are you going to look for in Atlanta?" her friend asked.

"I don't know. I've never really looked around Atlanta. I attended a conference there once for two days. The people were very friendly."

"And you decided on the spur of the moment to move there? Because we aren't friendly here?"

"No, of course not! But if I had to leave, I thought—I mean, a change of place can be very invigorating."

"So how many times have you moved before?"

Diane felt her cheeks heat up. "None."

"None? You lived in the fourplex all your life?"

"No. I moved there after college."

"Where did you go to college?"

"Dallas, at SMU."

"Maybe it is time you moved," Elizabeth said with a gentle smile, "But I wish you hadn't decided to do it now."

Diane saw the tears Elizabeth was blinking away, and her own eyes filled. She reached out a hand to her friend. "I wish that, too. But I'll call you and give you my address, once I know it. I promise, Elizabeth. But you can't give it to anyone. Not even Mark."

"Why?" her friend asked.

"I—I don't want anyone to know."

"But, Diane, we could come visit you, or I could come by myself. But I'd have to leave your number with Mark. I can't abandon him with the kids and not give him a number to call if he gets in trouble."

"No, I guess you couldn't," Diane agreed. But she knew now that she couldn't confide in Elizabeth. And she guessed it wasn't fair to even ask her to keep something from her husband.

"When will you reach Atlanta?"

"I think I may take three days. That will still give me the weekend to find an apartment to rent."

Elizabeth didn't seem to have any more questions. Diane guessed she didn't have any more answers, either. They both sat silently, eating their pancakes.

Until Diane's stomach revolted.

She left the table and ran for the restroom.

Elizabeth stared after her, a smile finding its way to her lips.

She looked suitably worried when Diane arrived back at the table. "Are you all right? I would've come after you, but both our purses were here, and I didn't know what to do."

"I'm fine. I just needed to—um, to go to the bathroom. I'm sorry if I startled you."

"I'm just glad you're all right. But I can see why you're losing weight. Maybe you should go back to your doctor."

"No. He said it would take the pills a little time to become effective."

"Well, maybe you should try to eat the rest of your pancakes."

Diane shuddered. "I think I'll just drink my tea."

"Okay, if you're sure."

After they finished their breakfast and Elizabeth paid the bill, insisting it be her treat, they got back in the car.

Diane thought her friend was driving slowly. "Is anything wrong, Elizabeth?"

"No. Why do you ask?"

"We're not going very fast. I don't mean to rush you, but I need to get started."

Just then, Elizabeth's cell phone rang. "Hello? Oh,

hi, Mark. Oh really? All right, I'm just taking Diane home. Yes, I'll see you then."

"Are you going to have lunch with Mark?" Diane asked.

"Maybe. He took the day off to look after the kids today. I'm having a minivacation."

"What a nice idea. That's sweet of Mark."

"Yes, he really is a good guy, in spite of being a dull banker!" Elizabeth said with a laugh.

They didn't speak again until Elizabeth pulled into the parking lot at the fourplex. "Oh, look, there's the mover's van," she exclaimed.

"Yes," Diane said, suddenly overcome with sadness. She didn't want to leave. But she couldn't stay. She had to cut her ties here, all of them.

Diane opened her door and got out. Elizabeth came around the car and hugged her.

When she released her, Diane spun around to go to her own car. Only she ran into a large mountain named John.

Chapter Fifteen

Diane gasped and nearly fell back against Elizabeth's car. She was supposed to have left already, been on the road, when John returned.

He grabbed her when she wobbled. "I didn't mean to startle you," he said with a grin that lit up his eyes.

"I—I'm just surprised, that's all. I thought you weren't coming back until tonight." Her voice sounded as breathless as she felt.

"A lucky break, then, huh?" He leaned down and kissed her. Right in front of Elizabeth and the movers, he wrapped his arms around her and claimed her.

Before she could stop herself, Diane kissed him back. It was a kiss goodbye, she told herself, rationalizing her actions. After all, she'd never be able to do this again, to press her body against his like this. Not when she was leaving him.

When his lips left hers, he finally noticed the moving van. "Who's moving out? Is it Jennifer? I've heard so much about her, I'd love to meet her."

"No!" Diane answered sharply. Then she stated in a calmer voice, "It's not Jennifer. She and Nick and the kids already moved."

"It's the flight attendant, then." He appeared relieved. "Now at least they'll stop chasing me."

Diane wasn't about to correct him. Let him think that. It'd get her off the hook. But she didn't have time to relax as the ground beneath her seemed to shift, the car behind her seemed to spin. Or was it her?

"Are you all right?" John asked. "You suddenly don't look so good."

She drew in a deep breath and kept her gaze focused on the van. "I'm fine."

He tucked a finger under her chin, forcing her to look up at him. "Let's go upstairs so we can be alone."

"No!" she shrieked. "My—my apartment isn't clean. I—I haven't had time to straighten up."

"It's just me, Diane," he said. "I promise I won't mind. I want to be with you."

She could feel herself panicking, her heart rate picking up. "No, I'd be horrified."

John relented. "Okay, then let's go to my house. We can have lunch with Gladys and Mildred and then go up to my room."

"I can't. I have to clean my apartment."

He looked at her as if she was being irrational. "Then I'll help you."

"No!" Once again, the world was spinning too fast around her, and she could feel sweat beading on her forehead.

John looked over her shoulder to see Elizabeth standing there quietly. "Can you get a cleaning lady to take care of Diane's apartment? It'll be my treat."

"No!" Diane exclaimed sharply. "No one is going up to my apartment except me. It's my mess and I'll clean it up."

"Calm down, honey. I'm just trying to get some time alone with you. We haven't had much the past week."

"And whose fault is that?" The words were out before she could stop them. She didn't want to have this conversation. She just wanted to go without making it harder.

"I know. I've been dealing with some things."

"You mean, other than your dad dying? What else?"

For a moment he didn't answer. His eyes searched hers. "I've been wanting you so badly, and I thought the feeling would go away if I held back." He took her by the shoulders. "But it didn't. I still need you more than ever, Diane."

"I don't believe you!" She couldn't. She was leaving. Her head started to pound, to spin again.

"You kissed me like you believed me!" he retorted, losing his calm.

"Go away, John! I can't deal with you right now!" She broke free, but was too dizzy to move.

"No, I won't go away! You've got to deal with me!"

But as he finished his words, the ground went out from under her and she sank toward the pavement. John reached out and caught her just before she fell. Her took her in his arms, saying "Diane? Diane, answer me."

But she was unconscious.

He looked to Elizabeth, who'd run to his side. "I'm taking her upstairs," he said, turning toward the fourplex.

Elizabeth stopped him. "You can't. They're packing up her apartment. Take her to our house."

Her words didn't register. They were packing Diane's apartment. Why? He banished the questions and dealt with the woman in his arms.

John carried her to his car and laid her down on the back seat. She never opened her eyes. He slid behind the wheel and started the engine, turning the air-conditioning on full force. As he was backing out, he called Gladys on his cell phone.

"I'm bringing Diane to the house," he told her. "She needs a bed prepared for her."

"What's wrong with her?"

"I don't know. She passed out."

"Get her here quickly, John."

That was what he intended to do. It suddenly occurred to him that Elizabeth seemed to know what was going on. Had Diane told her what was wrong with her?

John pressed his foot on the accelerator. Three minutes later, he pulled into his driveway.

Sliding her out of the car into his arms, he strode across the front lawn and leaned on the doorbell. When Gladys had opened the door, she immediately led him up the stairs to the first bedroom on the right. The covers had been turned down on the bed. Gladys quickly removed her shoes and helped tuck her in.

"What caused her to pass out?" she whispered.

"We were having a—an argument," John admitted, his head bowed. "She wouldn't go up to her apartment with me. She said it was dirty."

"You shouldn't have pushed her," Gladys said. "Maybe she didn't get enough sleep last night."

He shook his head. "All I know is that I'm staying with her. She won't know where she is when she comes to."

But the front doorbell diverted his attention. "That will be Mark and Elizabeth. I think Elizabeth knows what's wrong with her." John turned and ran down the stairs. He threw open the door and welcomed his friends inside.

"Elizabeth, do you know what's wrong with Diane?"

She lowered her eyes. "Not for sure, but she said she went to the doctor because she was losing weight. This morning she took a vitamin the doctor had prescribed for her."

"So she passed out because she's not eating enough? Didn't you take her to breakfast?"

"I did," Elizabeth said, then paused, as if trying to think of what to say. "She didn't eat much."

"You know something you're not telling me!" John accused. Even her husband was staring at her suspiciously.

"No, I don't!" Elizabeth exclaimed. "She didn't tell me what was wrong and she didn't explain why she was leaving."

John speared her with his gaze. "But you've figured it out, haven't you?"

GLADYS TIPTOED into the darkened room. When she got to the bed, she gently shook Diane's shoulder to see if she would open her eyes.

After a moment, her eyelashes fluttered.

"Diane, it's Gladys. You're in John's house because you passed out. Is there anything I can do for you?"

"Is John here?" At Gladys's nod, she tried to sit up, but the housekeeper held her back. "Don't let him come up here. I don't want to see him."

"Don't worry, honey, I won't let him come in, not until you say so. Meanwhile I brought you some fresh lemonade."

"Thank you, Gladys."

With her help, Diane sat up and took a drink. Then she ate some of the oatmeal cookies the woman had brought, and drank more lemonade. But the action seemed to exhaust her, and she finally leaned back and murmured, "I think I want to sleep now."

"Of course, dear. Sleep as long as you want." Tucking the blanket around Diane, she tiptoed out of the room.

As soon as she reached the kitchen, John turned away from his conversation with Elizabeth. "Gladys, did you check on Diane?"

"Yes, she's sleeping nicely now. I think she must not've gotten much rest recently."

"I guess that could be, but—" John suddenly remembered Diane not answering her phone when he'd tried to call back last night. Had she gone out for the evening, perhaps?

He looked at Elizabeth. "Was she seeing anyone else?"

The woman stared at him. "When would she have had time?"

"I wasn't in the picture much last week."

"And you think Diane is the kind of person who must be entertained all the time? Who can't handle being without a date on a Saturday night?"

"No, but something's going on."

"Obviously, since she's moving," Elizabeth retorted. "But you'll have to ask her what's happening. Quit asking us to guess. That's not fair to Diane."

"She's moving?" Gladys asked in surprise.

"Yeah. She quit her job and called a moving company yesterday. She's going to Atlanta."

Gladys opened her mouth to speak but then turned away, supposedly to help Mildred with the sandwiches she was taking out of the oven.

John pressed her. "Gladys, did Diane tell you anything?"

"Only that she needed to sleep."

He turned and slumped into a chair. "What am I going to do?"

"There's no reason you can't go to Atlanta, too," Elizabeth suggested carefully watching his facial expression. "I mean, she'll be at the same bank, only in that city."

"So I should chase after her when she's made it clear she wants nothing to do with me?"

Elizabeth said softly, "I thought you loved her."

"I never said that!" John growled.

"Maybe you should. Maybe you should figure out

what you want and what Diane wants. Then you'd know if it would be worth whatever she wants to keep her."

"What do *you* want?" Mark asked John. "Women like Diane, and Elizabeth, expect more than a few tosses in the hay before you walk away. She's trusted you and let you have your way with her. She's played by your rules. So you have no room to complain. If you want to change the rules, you'll have to let her know."

John got up and started pacing. "I've been thinking about it. But I wanted her so badly after my father's death, I forced myself to stay away. Don't you see? If I love her, then she has the upper hand. She can do whatever she wants and I can't say no! I'd be losing control."

Mark actually laughed. "Yeah. I lost control, too. And I've never been happier." He clapped his friend on the back. "It makes you human, John. Waking up to the same woman never gets dull. And at night, when we tuck the kids in bed, they put their arms around our necks and tell us they love us. It's a great thing. I wouldn't trade it for anything."

The mention of children, put John on overload. "No one's mentioned kids!" he snapped.

Gladys set a plate in front of John. "Maybe someone should."

"What do you mean?"

"I don't mean anything, but to your daddy, you were the best thing that came from his marriage to your mom. Unfortunately, she didn't live long, but Mildred tells me he really loved you and your mom."

"Yeah, but he didn't pay much attention to my brothers."

"That's because he hated their mommas. Do you hate Diane?"

"Of course not!"

"Do you love her?"

"I'm not prepared to say that!"

Mark interrupted. "But you want *her* to say she loves *you?*"

"I thought it was fair to find out where I stand."

"I guess she answered you," Elizabeth said quietly.

"What do you mean?" John seemed ready to jump across the table.

"She's moving, isn't she?"

"If I've done something so bad that leaving is the only way she can respond, I need to know what it is." He turned to go upstairs to Diane, but Gladys stopped him with a hand on his arms.

"You can't go up, John. She asked me to keep you out of that room."

His eyes flashed with anger. "How dare she! It's my house!"

Gladys held her ground. "I promised," she said calmly.

"So I guess she said a little more than you told me earlier."

Caught in her lie, Gladys averted her eyes. "Yes, she did, but not much more. She said she needed to rest, and to please not let you come in."

"I think maybe we should call a doctor."

"I know the doctor she went to see yesterday morning," Elizabeth interjected. "He won't tell you anything confidential, but he'd let you know if you should bring her in."

"Why didn't you say so?" John demanded.

"You mustn't try to force him to tell you what's wrong."

"I'll let you talk to him. Fair enough?"

"Okay." Elizabeth pulled out her cell phone and checked the number. During one of their dinner conversations, she and Diane had discovered they shared the same doctor. Now she dialed the number and asked for the nurse.

Elizabeth explained what had happened, and then asked if the doctor needed to see Diane.

"Did she hit her head?" the nurse asked.

"No."

"Has she spoken since she passed out?"

"Yes, but she went back to sleep."

"She should be all right. She just needs lots of rest right now. Let her sleep as long as she wants."

"Yes, of course."

Elizabeth hung up the phone and said, "The nurse says she's fine. Just let her sleep."

Gladys breathed a sigh of relief.

John, however, was not satisfied. "Why didn't you talk to the doctor? She could have something terribly wrong with her."

"I promise you the nurse knows or she would have consulted the doctor. But if Diane shows other symptoms than she has so far, we can call back."

"Why don't we follow the nurse's advice and let her sleep," Gladys proposed. "I have a feeling she'll be out for hours. You might as well go about your work," she said to John. "I'll take good care of her."

"You won't let her leave? She'll start her drive to Atlanta if you do."

"No, I won't let her do that."

John nodded. "I do need to check on my projects."

Mark stood. "And I need to check in with my office. Elizabeth, you want me to drive you home first?"

Gladys hurriedly said, "She could stay and have another glass of lemonade. I'll take her home when she wants to go."

Once the two men had left, Gladys brought Elizabeth more lemonade and she and Mildred joined her at the table to eat their own sandwiches. They ate in silence until Gladys blurted, "I think she's pregnant."

"But she said she's on birth control pills," Elizabeth said cautiously.

Gladys shrugged. "The Davis men are virile, and Doug was certainly potent. And pregnancy is the only reason I can see for her to run away."

"What happened at breakfast?" Mildred asked.

"Everything was fine. I teased her about not drinking coffee. But she said she was wide-awake and didn't need coffee. Then, suddenly, her eyes widened and she jumped up and ran for the bathroom. For a second I thought she *was* pregnant."

"Is that the first time she's thrown up?" Gladys asked.

"I don't know. But it may be why she went to the doctor."

"Makes sense. She's never been around a pregnant woman."

"She hasn't," Elizabeth agreed. "Her parents weren't much in the picture during her childhood. And Mark says she never sees them."

Mildred shook her head. "It's a shame. She's a very sweet young lady. When she came to dinner, Angi was her usual difficult self, but that didn't phase Diane. She let Angi do her worst and just smiled at her. It made my heart feel good. And Doug was really impressed with her. He told me he thought John had finally found his woman."

"Not if he doesn't realize it," Elizabeth muttered.

"True. And if she is pregnant and she goes away, we'll never see the baby. Worse, she'll be taking care of the child all alone. You know a new mother needs help. It breaks my heart to think she's going away."

The others shared Mildred's concern and quiet reigned for the remainder of lunch, until they heard someone on the stairs.

Gladys jumped up from her chair and rushed toward the kitchen door.

"Diane! How are you feeling?"

"I'm fine. And I appreciate your letting me rest here without—without John coming in."

"Of course, if that's what you needed. Come, let me fix you some lunch. You need something in your stomach." She urged Diane into the kitchen.

Diane was surprised to see Elizabeth. "What are you doing here?" she asked.

"I'm enjoying my free day. How are you feeling?"

"I feel fine. I just needed a little sleep."

"And some food," Gladys interjected. She and Mildred turned to heat her up a sandwich.

"Lunch was wonderful. You'll love it," Elizabeth told Diane.

"I'm not sure—"

But Gladys cut her off. "You have to eat something, Diane." She shot a quick, daring look at the others, then added, "For the baby."

Chapter Sixteen

Diane gasped and her cheeks betrayed her, reddening instantly. Still she feigned ignorance. "What baby?"

"We've all figured it out, honey," Gladys said. "And we don't want you to go away. We can help you."

Diane looked from one woman to the next, meeting their eyes. It was no use. She'd never been a good liar. "You can't help me," she finally admitted. "If I stay here, John will ask me to get rid of the baby, and I can't do that!"

"Of course you can't," Mildred agreed, coming over to hug her. "And we won't let him suggest such a thing."

"You can't stop him, Mildred. He's always said no children, no marriage. Those were his conditions. I thought I was protected because I take birth control pills for my skin. At least I did. But my doctor said they probably weren't strong enough." She sighed, trying to maintain her control. "I have to leave if I'm keeping the baby. John mustn't know."

"But I think he should know," Elizabeth said.

"No, I can't tell him. Once he knows, he'll always feel badly about our—our time together."

Elizabeth shook her head. "I think you're underestimating John."

Mildred frowned. "What do you mean?"

"You're all assuming John wouldn't want her to have the baby. But given the choice of having Diane or not having Diane, I think he'd marry her in a minute."

"And if he doesn't?" Diane asked, her voice wobbly.

"Then you'd be no worse off than you are now, but you'd have three friends willing to help you." Elizabeth gave her a warm smile.

"You mean I should stay here?"

"Why not?"

"But I couldn't involve the three of you in my baby's life."

"I don't know why not," Gladys assured her. "I work for John but he doesn't own me!"

"I don't even work for him," Mildred said. "I could live with you and take care of the baby while you go to work."

"That would be wonderful, Mildred, but I don't have a job or a place to live!" Diane covered her face with her hands. "I've messed everything up!"

"You were just trying to protect your child, Diane. That's never wrong," Elizabeth said softly.

"If I could get my job back, I could buy a house and Mildred and I could move in. That would be terrific." For the first time in a long time, Diane smiled.

"Call the bank at once," Elizabeth recommended.

"Mr. Harvey's not going to like it," she said, wiping the smile off her face.

"If he hasn't found anyone yet, I bet he'll be relieved."

Diane made the phone call. Mr. Harvey was hesitant at first, but when she revealed that she was pregnant, he took her back at once. His own wife had become irrational during her pregnancies, he explained, so he understood.

Diane hung up the phone, after asking to have the rest of the week off, and grinned at her coconspirators. "Okay, I have my job back. Won't Wendy be surprised!"

"So will John," Elizabeth said. "But I think he'll like it."

Mildred beamed at her. "And I have a house for you to look at. I've been kind of waiting to see how much money I'd have, but you might want to buy this house yourself. Why don't you go look at it? It's empty."

"Where is it?"

"Just a couple of blocks away."

Eager to start her new life, Diane asked, "Can we go now?"

"Let me call the Realtor."

Within minutes, the four of them got in Elizabeth's car and drove the two blocks to a neat, two-story house set back from the road.

"It's not as big as Doug's or John's place, but it's got four bedrooms, three baths."

"It sounds perfect," Diane said.

When the Realtor arrived, he showed them through the house. When he'd finished the tour, he asked if there were any questions. Diane had a lot, which proved she knew what she was doing.

"Are you some kind of economist?" he asked.

"No, I'm a banker."

"Oh. What bank?"

"Guaranty National."

"Hey, this house went in bankruptcy. I think it's your bank that owns it."

"Perfect," Diane said with a smile. Maybe it was meant to be.

After they got back to John's house, Diane called the man in charge of real estate at the bank to talk about the house. When she got off the phone, she said, "I've bought it."

"Just like that?" Elizabeth asked in astonishment.

"Yes. They know my credit rating and all the financials. They offered it to me below market price, and I accepted."

"When do you get the keys?" Gladys asked.

"Whenever I want them. I need to call the mover and give him the new address."

When they all offered to help move her things in tomorrow, she grinned at the women. "You've each been so helpful."

"That's what friends are for," Gladys said. "And I'm so happy that Mildred will be close to me. She's my best friend. And we'll both take good care of you, Diane."

Diane's eyes filled with tears. "I've always taken care of myself, but I'll admit that I feel a little better now. I don't know what it's like being pregnant."

"And that's where I come in," Elizabeth said. "You

can call me and ask questions about anything. I'll be able to tell you whether you need to call the doctor."

"Oh, that's wonderful!" Diane sank back in her chair. "The only problem will be John."

"He won't be a problem. He'll be on his knees, begging you to accept him. I'm sure of that. He's always a bear when he hasn't seen you for a while," Gladys told her.

"That doesn't mean he loves me."

Gladys had started to reply when they heard the front door open.

Elizabeth reached out and squeezed Diane's hand in a show of support, but still Diane tensed, waiting to see John.

"Gladys?" he called.

"We're in the kitchen," she replied.

"Has Diane woken up yet?" John asked as he came through the doorway, and then came to an abrupt halt when he saw her sitting at the table. Behind him, Mark nearly ran into his back.

John was silent for an awkward moment before he asked, "How are you feeling, Diane?"

"Fine. Thank you for bringing me here. The rest helped." She affected a casual tone, but that couldn't be further from what she was feeling.

"I'm glad. Uh, we called your doctor's office to see if you were all right or needed to be checked out, but the nurse said you were okay."

"Yes, thank you."

Then, as if he couldn't hold his feelings in any

longer, he erupted in exasperation. "What the hell is going on with you? Why are you leaving?"

"I'm not. Not anymore."

He took a deep breath. "Well, that's good. Why *were* you leaving?"

"I don't think you want to know."

He ran a hand through his hair. "Okay, so we just go on as we have been?"

"No, that's not possible."

"You're not making sense, Diane. If you're not leaving, there's no reason we can't go on as before. Unless you're making demands on me."

"No, John. I'm not making demands on you." She kept her gaze down on the table. She didn't want him to see the tears that glistened in her eyes.

"Why aren't you?" he asked.

She gathered her emotions and looked him right in the eyes, her straight posture echoing the staunch words. "You told me you didn't want any demands made on you. That you didn't allow that. You said I had to play by your rules. I'm doing that, John."

As if finally realizing they were having this intimate discussion in the middle of a crowd of people, John barked, "Why are you all here listening? Don't you have something to do?"

Gladys spoke for all of them. "Diane is our friend and we've offered to help her work out her problems."

John stood there, his hands on his hips, scowling at all of them. "That's what I've been offering to do, but she won't tell me the problem." He turned to

Diane, clearly frustrated. "Why do they all get to know and I don't?"

Diane raised her chin. "Because they aren't going to be mad at me. You are."

"No, I won't!" John roared.

Want to make a bet? an inner voice mocked. What she was about to tell him would rock him.

She drew a deep breath and gave him what he wanted—the truth.

"Fine, I'll tell you. I went to the doctor yesterday to find out why I was throwing up so often and losing weight." She swallowed past the knot in her throat. "And he told me I was pregnant."

HE MUST BE HALLUCINATING. He could've sworn he heard her say she was pregnant. His eyes searched hers, begging her to set him straight. "You're what?"

"I'm pregnant, John."

How could she be so calm, so matter-of-fact? He wondered. His own heart threatened to explode in his chest as one word kept pounding in it. Pregnant.

Diane spoke when he couldn't find the words. "I know you don't want children, but I'm going to have the baby. So I thought it would be better for me to leave and move to a town where I didn't know anyone. But my friends have convinced me to stay here and have my child."

"Here? In this house?" John stared at her.

"No, John, not in your house," she said softly. "Never in your house." She stood and looked at Gladys. "Thank you for the shelter and the encouragement. Mildred, come when you're ready. Elizabeth, thanks for being there for me."

"Wait, where are you going?" John demanded. Surely she didn't think she could drop a bomb like this and just walk away.

But Diane didn't even hesitate. She started to walk out, then stopped suddenly. "I don't have my car here. Elizabeth, would you and Mark mind dropping me off?"

"Of course we will." Elizabeth didn't give her husband time to say anything. She put her arm around Diane and led her out of the house.

Left standing there, helpless, with Gladys and Mildred, John could only ask, "What just happened here?"

Gladys gave him an exasperated look. "She told you the truth and you behaved just as she predicted. I'm very disappointed in you, John." She began clearing the table, turning her back on him.

"Hey! She broke one of my rules! I told her I didn't want to have babies."

"You need to think about someone other than yourself, boy," Mildred said. "She was alone and scared. Willing to move a long way away and start over again to protect her child. That wasn't an easy choice."

"Why is everyone mad at me? I didn't mislead her. I told her before we started our affair exactly how I felt." He looked to the two women, but Gladys didn't answer him and Mildred left the room.

Great, he thought. He'd lost not only Diane, but the only other women in his life.

John dropped into a chair and leaned his elbows on the table in front of him. He put his head in his hands and moaned, "What do I do now?"

AFTER TALKING TO the movers at the fourplex, Diane pulled out of Yellow Rose Lane for the last time. She drove to a nice hotel and got a room. She'd promised to have the key for the movers by ten o'clock the next morning.

Then she drew a rough version of the floor plan of her new house and worked out where the furniture would fit. She wasn't sure about some of it, but she'd need more furniture, anyway. She couldn't ask Mildred to sleep on a sofabed. And, of course, she'd need to set up the nursery.

How soon would she know the sex of the child? She took out the brochures and learned it'd be a while yet. She had time to prepare the nursery. After all, when she got home from work now, she wouldn't have John in her life. Her time would be all her own again.

It'll be peaceful, she told herself.

It'll be lonely, replied her heart.

Once again tears welled in her eyes, and as much as she willed them back, they flowed freely down her cheeks.

She had to stop thinking about John. All the pregnancy brochures told her she needed to keep a positive attitude. And she would. For her baby.

And John's.

JOHN DIDN'T KNOW where Diane went for the night. He would've gladly put her up, but he wasn't given a choice. She simply walked out of his life.

He tossed and turned all night, picturing her pregnant, unprotected, with men hitting on her. She wouldn't know how to handle them. She didn't know much about men.

Where would she find a place to live? She might pick a place in a bad neighborhood. After all, now she had to be doubly careful.

Then he remembered he was talking about Diane. Intelligent, savvy, levelheaded Diane. She'd done fine on her own, had been on her own all her life.

Until he stepped into it.

He was the one who'd messed things up for her, threw a curve into the straight-arrow life she led. But he couldn't help it. Something about her drew him. He knew what it was. Her independence, her intelligence. They were what he loved about her.

Loved?

Yeah, loved, he admitted to himself. He loved Diane Black and it scared the hell out of him.

Now he didn't even know where to reach her, where to call. She wasn't at the fourplex anymore, but where had she gone? Damn it, he intended to get her a cell phone, but then his father had died and…

And he'd gotten cold feet.

Why had that happened? he asked himself. Then he remembered. He'd needed her too much. He'd thought if he spent some time away, he might get control of his need for her. Instead, he'd lost her completely.

Thinking over the day, he suddenly remembered Diane telling Mildred to come when she was ready. To come where? And what did she need to be ready for?

He was up early, dressed in jeans and a polo shirt, and ran down the stairs.

Only Gladys was in the kitchen.

"Good morning, Gladys. Uh, where is Mildred?"

"She's busy."

"Isn't she going to eat breakfast?"

"She ate earlier."

"She's sure up early. She must have a lot planned for today," he said, baiting his housekeeper.

"Yep."

"Gladys, what are you not telling me?"

She stopped stirring his scrambled eggs. "Mildred is moving out."

John frowned. "Why?"

"Because she's found something she likes better."

He folded his arms over his chest and asked, "What did she find?"

"You'll have to ask her," Gladys said.

John planned to do exactly that. He got up and went to the stairs to call her down.

"Yesterday, when Diane left, she told you to come when you were ready. What did she mean?" he asked when she appeared.

"Exactly what she said," Mildred replied.

John looked at her. "Mildred, I don't want to beg, but I need to know where to find Diane. I want a chance to talk to her."

"I'm moving in with Diane to help her with her pregnancy. The first three months are difficult because she will be nauseous and exhausted. The middle three months aren't too bad. We can fix up the house during that time. And the last three, she'll be so big it won't be any fun to move around."

"Damn! Why do women want to get pregnant if that's true?"

"Because they get the sweetest gift God can give. A baby."

John stared at Mildred's gentle smile. "You're going to help Diane?"

"Yes. She's never had anyone to rely on. I think that's wrong. I'm glad to take the place of her mother. I would be proud to have a daughter like her."

John put his arm around the woman. "Thank you, Mildred. That's a gift I couldn't give Diane. But I'm glad you can."

"But there is something *you* can do," Gladys called out.

John looked at her. "What?"

"You can tell her you'll love her son or daughter, because it will be yours, too." Gladys stared at him, waiting.

John didn't bother denying his love for Diane. He sank down at the table again. "I'm afraid, Gladys. If I let her know that I love her, that I'll love my child, she could demand anything of me. I'm not sure I can do that."

"John, think about Diane. Has she ever demanded anything of you?"

John sat there thinking for a minute. Then he looked up. "No, she hasn't. But she's never said she loved me, either."

"Did you tell her you loved her?"

"No, Gladys, I didn't because…because I was afraid."

"I think your father would tell you to trust your instincts. Diane is a good woman—and the mother of your child."

John stared first at Gladys and then at Mildred. "Do you think she loves me?"

"You need to muster your courage and ask her that," Gladys said.

As always, the woman was right. "I will. But where is she?"

"At the house she bought yesterday," Mildred replied.

"She bought a house yesterday?" John asked, astonished.

"Yes. I'd been looking at it for myself, but I thought she'd like it, and it was empty. I didn't know it was being handled by her bank."

"Are you talking about the house two streets over?" John asked.

Mildred nodded. "She's meeting the movers there at ten o'clock. I thought I'd go over and help her, you know, and make sure she doesn't overdo."

That was his job, John thought. A husband's job. A father's job.

Mildred looked at him with a gleam in her eye. "What are you doing today? Are you busy?"

He smiled back and stood up, ever grateful for these two women who meant so much to him. "I've got only one thing to do. Get my woman."

DIANE GOT TO HER HOUSE early. As much as she'd miss the fourplex, she loved the idea of having her own place. Four bedrooms. That meant she could have a guest room as well as the baby's room, Mildred's room, and hers.

She walked through the house, picturing her baby growing up here. Too bad she pictured John here, too.

She was berating herself for the errant thought when the doorbell rang. Figuring the movers had arrived early, she swung open the door.

To discover John.

"Hello," she managed to say.

"Hello, Diane." He smiled uneasily. "I hear we're going to be neighbors."

"I won't bother you. You don't have to worry."

His temper flared. "Damn it, Diane, I'm not worried about that!"

"Then why are you here?"

He glanced away and let out a breath. What seemed like hours later, he finally looked at her and said, "Because I love you, and I want to know if you love me."

She stared at him, wondering what he was up to now. "Of course I love you, but I won't change my mind about having my baby."

"*Our* baby. You aren't having this baby by yourself, you know."

"Yes, I am. I may not have gotten pregnant by myself, but I'm surely having the baby by myself!"

"And what if I say you aren't?" he growled.

"I don't see how it's any of your business, John. We aren't together anymore."

"Then I think we'll have to get married," he replied matter-of-factly. "Because I can't live without you now. And when our baby arrives, I won't be able to live without him or her, either."

Her blood rushed through her veins, throbbing so loud she couldn't trust her hearing. "John, what are you trying to say?" she asked, her voice trembling.

"I'm trying to say I love you, Diane. Please marry me. I can't let you go."

She stared at him. "You're sure?"

"Yes, I said I was."

There really was only one answer. There'd always been only one. "Yes, John, I'll marry you. But if you break my heart, I'll never forgive you," she said with a sob, and threw herself into his embrace.

John held her so tightly against him, she doubted he'd ever let her go. But that was fine with her.

Raining a trail of kisses down her neck, he whispered, "I want to make love to you right now, right here." He pressed her against the wall and claimed her mouth with a kiss that made her breathless.

When she was able to speak, she said, "But the movers are due here any minute."

He looked down at her. "So you've bought the house and are having your furniture moved in here?"

"Yes."

"But you'll live with me when we're married, won't you?"

"Of course. And what about Mildred! Will she be

able to live with us, too? She wants to take care of the baby."

He laughed. "We'll work everything out, sweetheart. I think Mildred might buy this house from you and just come to our place to care for the baby when it arrives, if you want to go back to work."

"I have to work!"

"You could handle your investments from home, couldn't you?"

"Yes, I guess I could. But I have to go back to the bank for a little while. After all, Mr. Harvey gave me my job back. He—"

John cut her off with a quick kiss. "I don't want to hear one more word about Mr. Harvey." He kissed her again, this time long and with emotion. "Now, we have other things to do." He lowered his head again, but the doorbell rang and Diane pulled back.

"That'll be the moving team." She went to the door and opened it. The movers greeted her and she let them in.

Soon she put John to work, too, helping move her furniture in.

"This wasn't what I had in mind when I came down here this morning," he muttered as he passed her by.

"I know, sweetheart, but I really don't have that much to move in. It'll just be a few more trips from the van to the house."

About that time, Mildred and Gladys came in, carrying bags of groceries. They both wore secret smiles when they saw Diane.

"Gladys, Mildred, we're going to get married," she

announced as soon as she saw them. "Isn't it wonderful?"

Gladys glanced at John like a proud parent, then back to Diane. "Did he tell you he loves you?"

"Yes," she said with a beaming smile.

John came in the door with a chair. "Oh, good. I'm glad you're here. I need to take Diane to my house for—for a nap. Can you keep an eye on the movers? We'll be back later."

"John, we can't do that! It would be rude," Diane cried.

He pulled her into his arms. "I've been good for an entire hour, after you told me you loved me, sweetheart. I've about reached the end of my patience."

Gladys and Mildred laughed out loud. "Go ahead, Diane. We're used to his impatience. But he'd better be good to you!" Gladys warned.

"Oh, he will be, Gladys. He'll be wonderful," Diane said with a brilliant smile as she walked out the door with John, hand in hand.

* * * * *

Watch for the next book in Judy Christenberry's
DALLAS DUETS series,
MOMMY FOR A MINUTE,
coming August 2007
only from Harlequin American Romance!

Mediterranean Nights

Join the guests and crew of
Alexandra's Dream, *the newest luxury ship*
to set sail on the romantic Mediterranean,
as they experience the
glamorous world of cruising.

A new Harlequin continuity series
begins in June 2007 with
FROM RUSSIA, WITH LOVE
by Ingrid Weaver

Marina Artamova books a cabin on
the luxurious cruise ship
Alexandra's Dream,
when she finds out that her orphaned
nephew and his adoptive father are aboard.
She's determined to be reunited with the boy...
but the romantic ambience of the ship
and her undeniable attraction
to a man she considers her enemy
are about to interfere with her quest!

Turn the page for a sneak preview!

Piraeus, Greece

"There she is, Stefan. Alexandra's Dream." David Anderson squatted beside his new son and pointed at the dark blue hull that towered above the pier. The cruise ship was a majestic sight, twelve decks high and as long as a city block. A circle of silver and gold stars, the logo of the Liberty Cruise Line, gleamed from the swept-back smokestack. Like some legendary sea creature born for the water, the ship emanated power from every sleek curve—even at rest it held the promise of motion. "That's going to be our home for the next ten days."

The child beside him remained silent, his cheeks working in and out as he sucked furiously on his thumb. Hair so blond it appeared white ruffled against his forehead in the harbor breeze. The baby-sweet scent unique to the very young mingled with the tang of the sea.

"Ship," David said. "Uh, *parakhod*."

From beneath his bangs, Stefan looked at the *Alexandra's Dream*. Although he didn't release his thumb, the corners of his mouth tightened with the beginning of a smile.

David grinned. That was Stefan's first smile this afternoon, one of only two since they had left the orphanage yesterday. It was probably because of the boat—according to the orphanage staff, the boy loved boats, which was the main reason David had decided to book this cruise. Then again, there was a strong possibility the smile could have been a reaction to David's attempt at pocket-dictionary Russian. Whatever the cause, it was a good start.

The liaison from the adoption agency had claimed that Stefan had been taught some English, but David had yet to see evidence of it. David continued to speak, positive his son would understand his tone even if he couldn't grasp the words. "This is her maiden voyage. Her first trip, just like this is our first trip, and that makes it special." He motioned toward the stage that had been set up on the pier beneath the ship's bow. "That's why everyone's celebrating."

The ship's official christening ceremony had been held the day before and had been a closed affair, with only the cruise-line executives and VIP guests invited, but the stage hadn't yet been disassembled. Banners bearing the blue and white of the Greek flag of the ship's owner, as well as the Liberty circle of stars logo, draped the edges of the platform. In the center, a group of musicians and a dance troupe dressed in traditional white folk costumes performed for the benefit of the *Alexandra's Dream*'s first passengers. Their audience was in a festive mood, snapping their fingers in time to the music while the dancers twirled and wove through their steps.

David bobbed his head to the rhythm of the mandolins. They were playing a folk tune that seemed vaguely familiar, possibly from a movie he'd seen. He hummed a few notes. "Catchy melody, isn't it?"

Stefan turned his gaze on David. His eyes were a striking shade of blue, as cool and pale as a winter horizon and far too solemn for a child not yet five. Still, the smile that hovered at the corners of his mouth persisted. He moved his head with the music, mirroring David's motion.

David gave a silent cheer at the interaction. Hopefully, this cruise would provide countless opportunities for more. "Hey, good for you," he said. "Do you like the music?"

The child's eyes sparked. He withdrew his thumb with a pop. *"Moozika!"*

"Music. Right!" David held out his hand. "Come on, let's go closer so we can watch the dancers."

Stefan grasped David's hand quickly, as if he feared it would be withdrawn. In an instant his budding smile was replaced by a look close to panic.

Did he remember the car accident that had killed his parents? It would be a mercy if he didn't. As far as David knew, Stefan had never spoken of it to anyone. Whatever he had seen had made him run so far from the crash that the police hadn't found him until the next day.

The event had traumatized him to the extent that he hadn't uttered a word until his fifth week at the orphanage. Even now he seldom talked.

David sat back on his heels and brushed the hair from Stefan's forehead. That solemn, too-old gaze locked with his, and for an instant, David felt as if he looked back in time at an image of himself thirty years ago.

He didn't need to speak the same language to understand exactly how this boy felt. He knew what it meant to be alone and powerless among strangers, trying to be brave and tough but wishing with every fiber of his being for a place to belong, to be safe, and most of all for someone to love him….

He knew in his heart he would be a good parent to Stefan. It was why he had never considered halting the adoption process after Ellie had left him. He hadn't balked when he'd learned of the recent claim by Stefan's spinster aunt, either; the absentee relative had shown up too late for her case to be considered. The adoption was meant to be. He and this child already shared a bond that went deeper than paperwork or legalities.

A seagull screeched overhead, making Stefan start and press closer to David.

"That's my boy," David murmured. He swallowed hard, struck by the simple truth of what he had just said.

That's my *boy*.

"I CAN'T BE PATIENT, RUDOLPH. I'm not going to stand by and watch my nephew get ripped from his country and his roots to live on the other side of the world."

Rudolph hissed out a slow breath. "Marina, I don't like the sound of that. What are you planning?"

"I'm going to talk some sense into this American kidnapper."

"No. Absolutely not. No offence, but diplomacy is not your strong suit."

"Diplomacy be damned. Their ship's due to sail at five o'clock."

"Then you wouldn't have an opportunity to speak with him even if his lawyer agreed to a meeting."

"I'll have ten days of opportunities, Rudolph, since I plan to be on board that ship."

* * * * *

*Follow Marina and David
as they join forces to uncover
the reason behind little Stefan's
unusual silence, and the secret behind
the death of his parents....*

Look for From Russia, With Love
*by Ingrid Weaver
in stores June 2007.*

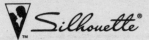

Silhouette®
Romantic
SUSPENSE

**Sparked by Danger,
Fueled by Passion.**

*This month and every month look for
four new heart-racing romances
set against a backdrop of suspense!*

Available in June 2007

Shelter from the Storm
by RaeAnne Thayne

A Little Bit Guilty
(Midnight Secrets miniseries)
by Jenna Mills

Mob Mistress
by Sheri WhiteFeather

A Serial Affair
by Natalie Dunbar

Available wherever you buy books!

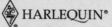
HARLEQUIN®

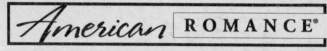
American ROMANCE®

**is proud to present a special treat this
Fourth of July with three stories
to kick off your summer!**

SUMMER LOVIN'
by
**Marin Thomas,
Laura Marie Altom
Ann Roth**

This year, celebrating the Fourth of July in Silver Cliff,
Colorado, is going to be special. There's an all-year
high school reunion taking place before the old
school building gets torn down. As old flames find
each other and new romances begin, this small
town is looking like the perfect place
for some summer lovin'!

*Available June 2007
wherever Harlequin books are sold.*

www.eHarlequin.com   HAR75169

REQUEST YOUR FREE BOOKS!
2 FREE NOVELS PLUS 2
FREE GIFTS!

American **ROMANCE**®

Heart, Home & Happiness!

YES! Please send me 2 FREE Harlequin American Romance® novels and my 2 FREE gifts. After receiving them, if I don't wish to receive any more books, I can return the shipping statement marked "cancel." If I don't cancel, I will receive 4 brand-new novels every month and be billed just $4.24 per book in the U.S., or $4.99 per book in Canada, plus 25¢ shipping and handling per book and applicable taxes, if any*. That's a savings of close to 15% off the cover price! I understand that accepting the 2 free books and gifts places me under no obligation to buy anything. I can always return a shipment and cancel at any time. Even if I never buy another book from Harlequin, the two free books and gifts are mine to keep forever.

154 HDN EEZK   354 HDN EEZV

Name _____ (PLEASE PRINT)

Address _____ Apt. #

City _____ State/Prov. _____ Zip/Postal Code

Signature (if under 18, a parent or guardian must sign)

Mail to the Harlequin Reader Service®:
IN U.S.A.: P.O. Box 1867, Buffalo, NY 14240-1867
IN CANADA: P.O. Box 609, Fort Erie, Ontario L2A 5X3

Not valid to current Harlequin American Romance subscribers.

Want to try two free books from another line?
Call 1-800-873-8635 or visit www.morefreebooks.com.

* Terms and prices subject to change without notice. NY residents add applicable sales tax. Canadian residents will be charged applicable provincial taxes and GST. This offer is limited to one order per household. All orders subject to approval. Credit or debit balances in a customer's account(s) may be offset by any other outstanding balance owed by or to the customer. Please allow 4 to 6 weeks for delivery.

Your Privacy: Harlequin is committed to protecting your privacy. Our Privacy Policy is available online at www.eHarlequin.com or upon request from the Reader Service. From time to time we make our lists of customers available to reputable firms who may have a product or service of interest to you. If you would prefer we not share your name and address, please check here. ☐

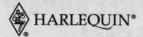

HARLEQUIN®

American **ROMANCE®**

COMING NEXT MONTH

**#1165 SUMMER LOVIN' by Marin Thomas, Laura Marie Altom
and Ann Roth**
This year, celebrating the Fourth of July in Silver Cliff, Colorado, is going
to be special. There's an all-year high school reunion taking place before the
school building gets torn down. As old flames find each other and new romances
begin, this season this small town is looking like the perfect place for some
summer lovin'!

#1166 THE COWGIRL'S CEO by Pamela Britton
Barrel-racing star Caroline Sheppard wants only one thing: to win the NFR,
the Super Bowl of rodeos. But she can't get there without help from millionaire
businessman Tyler Harrison. And his sponsorship comes with strings attached. But
even if Caro wants to turn him down, her heart, as Ty is about to learn, is as big
as the Wyoming sky....

#1167 THE MAN FOR MAGGIE by Lee McKenzie
Having distanced himself from his wealthy family, Nick Durrance started
his own construction business, and now pretty much keeps to himself. But
Maggie Meadowcroft sees something special in the man and decides to work
some magic on him to see if she can't reconnect him with his family and friends.
But when he starts falling for Maggie, things get really interesting!

#1168 HIS ONLY WIFE by Cathy McDavid
Aubrey Stuart is reluctant to get involved with hotshot firefighter
Gage Raintree. She loved him once, but now her life and her job as a nurse
is in Tucson, far away from the small town of Blue Ridge. At the end of the
summer she will have to leave—is the persistent Gage going to let her?

www.eHarlequin.com

HARCNM0507